DEATH OF OF ANGELS

Nerida E Marshall

S.T.A.R.S. Publishing
Australia

First published 2025
http://www.starsgc.com

A catalogue record for this
Book is available from the
NATIONAL   National Library of Australia
LIBRARY
OF AUSTRALIA

ISBN 978-0-646-71102-7

Cover design by Nerida E Marshall
Cover graphics by https://coxartworks.com.au

The author and publisher have made every effort to
contact holders of material used in this book. Any person
or organisation that may have been overlooked should
contact the publisher.

For my parents, whose research assistance uncovered many hidden or misfiled papers of importance.

The historical chapters of this book are fictional reconstructions of real events. All effort has been made to keep relevant facts accurate. It is based on the true outbreak of pneumonic plague in the port of Maryborough, Queensland, Australia in 1905.

CONSPIRACY OR PARANOIA?

After numerous attempts by the author searching through the Queensland Public Health Department files, no files could be located for Maryborough Hospital or the Colmslie Plague Hospital for the year 1905.

The author did find on public record that in June 1905 the Public Health Department of the day held a commission in the Maryborough Municipal Chambers to investigate deaths by pneumonic plague.

Behind a hospital door,

in the dim light of a passageway,

was a tablet in bronze, not easily seen.

It read:

Erected in memory of Nurse Rose A. Wiles

and Nurse Cecelia G. Bauer

who died while devotedly discharging

their duties in the service of the Institution

during June 1905.

'It could <u>not</u> have said less.'

Dr. P. A. Earnshaw

An important message from the author

It is my hope that this book will start

conversations on complete transparency and

truthfulness in all government medical issues

involving the community.

If you would like to see photographs and

information about the people involved in the

1905 outbreak please visit pages 194 – 203.

DAY ONE – Poverty and Illness
EMPIRE DAY, MAY 24, 1905.

'Plague would rush upon its victims with the
speed of fire racing through dry substances,'
Giovanni Boccaccio, *Decamero (1353)*

After a cursory rap on the rotting door, Doctor Crawford Robinson pushed it open and took a few measured steps inside. He immediately had cause to pull his carefully folded white handkerchief from his top pocket and place it quickly across his nose, 'Dear God in Heaven what a vile stench?' he exclaimed.

As the Maryborough Municipal Health Officer, it was his position to attend to those too poor to purchase medical attention. He was not a stranger in many homes of poverty and illness, despair and desperation. But none before this had been cloaked in such a putrid odor. Sounds of pain and vomiting were emanating from the dimness of the one room hovel.

His initial expression of distain melted slightly as he made out a young man groaning on the floor. Seventeen-year-old John O'Connell lay on his pathetic bed of hessian sacking soaked in urine, blood, and excrement. His stick thin arms were crossed over his stomach in a futile attempt to ease the racking pains.

'How long has he been like this?' Doctor Robinson demanded from the doorway.

Ellen O'Connell, at the tender age of seven, was sitting in

the filth cradling her brother's head, trying desperately to soothe him. Blood and other bodily fluids streaked her ashen face. Before she could answer John's groaning exploded into a coughing fit that resulted in volley after volley of thin watery sputum.

'Five days. He's been like this for five days,' from the shadows nine-year-old May O'Connell volunteered the information. She shyly walked towards him with one dirty hand clutching the arm of a grubby urchin-faced toddler with ringlets of rusty coloured hair, while her free arm cradled a sickly grey kitten.

'Well then, he is still alive, so it is probably another case of Dengue Fever, unpleasant, but not fatal. We are in the middle of an epidemic missy. Keep the fluids up to him and ah, well really, that is about all you can do.'

With that he strode quickly outside to gasp a breath of untainted air. He was going to tell the dirty-faced children to make their brother comfortable but thought better of it as he considered the lack of household necessities in the hut.

If the boy died the blame could be more accurately laid at the door of starvation and filth than any disease. What sane parent could leave children in such squalor he muttered to himself as he untied his horse from the broken front fence and jumped into his buggy.

PRESENT DAY 1 - MAY 24.

Cole Leedon took out a compass and a thin notebook,

'Hold on a second, Sue,' he drawled. 'That is truly some great storytelling but let me get my bearings. Now these horrific deaths started in May 1905?'

'That's right. You're standing on the very spot. It's a little eerie, isn't it?' Sue shivered slightly.

Sue James was a lanky freckly-faced woman of thirty-five years. As a volunteer with a local historical group, she had been diligently trying to gain national recognition for two nurses who had died caring for a tragic young family of pneumonic plague victims. The Black Death, as this plague was often called, had decimated populations from China to Italy to London over the course of human history. It was the most feared of all plagues and its pneumonic form was the deadliest and most virulent of them all. Radio, television, newspapers, magazines, if they would give her ten minutes, she would reveal a poignant piece of Australian history almost buried in over a century of neglect.

On the previous day an imposing foreigner had walked into Sue's historical group's temporary office and, in a gentle drawl, introduced himself,

'Cole Leedon is my name. On television recently I saw one of your group, Sue James, I would like to speak with her, if I may.'

His indefinable accent had a pleasing lilt with an undercurrent almost of a southern drawl. But as polite as he was his ramrod straight back and world-weary countenance made him a commanding presence.

Someone yelled unceremoniously, 'Sue, you're wanted out front.'

Sue came out from the kitchenette and saw a tall, well-built man waiting for her. Forty years ago, he would have been a heartbreaker, even now, pushing sixty at a guess; there was an excitement about him. His fair, collar length hair was quite grey at the temples, and he was dressed in expensive denim with the most ornate boots she'd ever come across.

'Sue? How are you? My name is Cole Leedon,' he shook her hand. It was warm and firm not crushing like a man with something to prove and not limp as if the courtesy was a waste of time.

'Sue, I am hoping that you might assist me with my research.' His intelligent green eyes were intense and watchful.

'It is my wish to reconstruct events surrounding the pneumonic plague outbreak here in 1905. I am particularly interested in the lives of the victims. This, I understand, is a specialty of yours. I will pay you an hourly rate and you choose the time. But one thing must be clear; I have an intractable deadline.'

Sue looked at him blankly.

He bent forward slightly as if in apology, 'My research must be completed by a date, already set, that cannot, for any reason be extended.'

'Are you a journalist or something, Mr. Leedon?'

'Nothing so glamorous, I am a Medical Researcher. My present project is compiling information on outbreaks of pneumonic plague around the world. Over the centuries it has flared up for no definable reason, changing the outcome of wars and world politics only to retreat back into dormancy. I am trying to determine what conditions cause a latent epidemic to re-activate.' He handed her a thin leather briefcase, 'References. Feel free to check them.'

'OK. Well, Mr. Leedon, I have two boys at school, providing we can work around that I could really use the extra cash.'

Cole nodded, 'On the television interview you said that the first case occurred on May 24, 1905. This is correct?'

'Yes, today is May twenty-three so the series of events actually started from tomorrow over a century ago.'

'You mentioned the dates on the television. That is why I am here now. It would be helpful to record the weather conditions as close as possible to the time of the outbreak. If you are agreeable, we will start in the morning. I have traveled a long way, and I am short on time. My card is in the briefcase. Kindly telephone me tonight with your answer. Good day.'

Sue turned to face her amazed colleagues, 'What about that? Maybe those TV interviews will pay off after all.'

*

At nine am the next morning Cole was leaning against a massive red four-wheel drive. His fitted jeans and blue shirt of the finest cotton were casual but designer cut. As Sue's undercoat grey Holden ground to a halt, she gave her new employer a once over behind her sunglasses. I'll bet he didn't buy those clothes off a hanger and those fancy boots, wow, I've never seen anything like them, even at the rodeos.

'Good morning, Sue,' Cole creaked open the car door for her. 'I am glad you telephoned last night. So, this is the site of the first death, correct?'

Sue pulled up the pants of her worn black tracksuit as she got out of the car, 'Yea, the corner of Sussex and Pallas Street.'

Cole looked at his compass and wrote the findings in a small notebook that he kept in his breast pocket.

'You scared of getting lost or something?' Sue asked.

'You mean the compass? Over the years I have learned to be meticulous the first time when researching a topic then there are no mistakes later.'

Sue shrugged a shoulder and carried on with her story, 'OK then. Now try and imagine a small timber hut on this spot. That's what was here in those days. Seven children lived here in utter squalor. Their mother had been dead for eighteen months. Their father, Richard O'Connell, worked at the wharves and it was rumored that he took to the drink after his wife died. Seventeen-year-old John O'Connell was the first to get the disease. Apparently, it was a horrific death.'

Cole lifted a tanned finger to indicate he was going to interrupt, 'It still is, you know. Pneumonic plague is not a dead disease. There are fatalities globally each year. Sorry to interrupt you Sue but I imagine that you are interested in all the facts about this disease. But back to your story; did the medical guys know they were dealing with pneumonic plague?'

Sue was a bit put off by his change of subject but was able to competently answer his question, 'There were so many epidemics in those days. John's death certificate says it was a severe case of Dengue Fever. Maryborough was suffering an epidemic at the time. Doctor Crawford Robinson attended John and considered the possibility of plague because two people had died of that disease two weeks earlier in a town called Childers about sixty-four kilometers away. Also, in Maryborough itself, two people had died of bubonic plague twelve months earlier.'

Cole nodded and commented, 'Bubonic plague could not be mistaken. Lymph glands in the groin and under the arm swell up like tennis balls. Usually there are large numbers of dead and dying rats around as well.'

'They were very aware of that. But according to the records there were no large numbers of dead or dying rats.' As they spoke Cole printed snippets in his notebook, 'This afternoon, Sue, I will study the newspaper clippings you have given me. And please remind me, what was the name of that other material that you want me to read?'

'*Unwept, Unhonour'd and Unsung*, by Dr. P.A. Earnshaw,' offered Sue. 'It's a paper he presented to the Medical Journal of Australia about this particular outbreak. You have a copy in the folder I gave you.'

'Thank you, Sue, you have thought of everything. So, there had never been cases of pneumonic plague in this country before?'

'None that we know of and nothing in the records that I could find,' answered Sue.

By now Cole was flicking through the plague notes as he carried on his questions, 'Where did the authorities say it come from then?'

Sue launched into the rumors and hearsay that had surrounded this very question for over a century, 'Richard

O'Connell, the father, worked on the wharves. Maryborough was one of the largest shipping ports in Queensland at the time. When he turned to drink after the death of his wife, he pretty much left the children to run wild. It was said that they played in the sewers and survived on handouts from kindly neighbors and whatever they could scavenge from around the local stores.'

Cole flicked his notebook cover and asked almost impatiently, 'So where did this plague come from?'

'I am getting to that, Cole. You need to understand the background first. One theory is that the father took hessian sacking from the hull of a ship recently in from Hong Kong and dragged it home for his children to use as bedding. Reports said that Hong Kong was in the grip of a terrible plague epidemic at the time, so the paper picked up on that snippet and reported that it came from there. But if that was the case and this disease is so contagious why didn't the father catch it himself?'

Cole's sea green eyes sparkled with interest, 'If the sacking was wet, which it probably was if it had come out of a freighter hull, then the bacterium could have been dormant. It dried out; the boy slept on it and breathed it in straight into the lungs making it a primary infection. It ties together. A secondary infection for pneumonic plague is caused when bubonic infection is left untreated and moves into the lungs. It does not seem to be the case here. What was the name of this ship?'

Sue shrugged her shoulder again. A habit, Cole thought to himself that could be rather irritating with time.

'The newspapers don't say,' she replied.

'Well, that is a great shame. I have spent quite some time

studying the 1905 plague in Hong Kong. It was a very nasty episode. With the name of a ship, I may have been able to fit in some missing pieces.'

Cole looked at his watch, 'Ah, I must finish some business elsewhere now. Shall we meet up here again tomorrow at the same time? We can then go over the first death.'

Sue nodded and Cole walked to her car. He even wrestled with her obstinate car door to open it for her. As she dropped into her worn car seat her attention was again caught by his extraordinary boots. Engraved gold leaf encased the heel and the toe, while gold thread traced the carvings in the black and red leather.

Cole followed her gaze, 'Only one pair like them in the world, one day I will tell you the story,' he said, rather mysteriously.

Sue slammed her car door shut muttering, 'Yea? I'd love to hear that story.'

To Cole she said, 'See you tomorrow.'

As she drove off Sue remarked to herself, jeez, some blokes are weird.

*

Cole walked into his motel room and threw the car keys casually onto the nearest bed, 'Chappie, is there any news?'

Chaplin Noel Howard, or Chappie to most people, popped his leathery tanned face around the bathroom door, 'An email from Lurman for you.'

As a big-boned, sinewy teen from the wilds of the Kimberley region he had drunk and fought his way around Australia until a near-death knife incident bought him close to God. Now he was a cynical world-weary Chaplin who found no surprises in any war-torn country or poverty-stricken village where his work led him. He was as meticulous a record keeper as Cole, but his temperament was as fiery as Cole's was calculating. They worked well together.

Cole hit the Inbox button on his laptop, 'Sender: Lurman. I have secured my position in a civilian hotel. I am ready to receive your instructions. End.'

Cole replied immediately, 'A reconstruction of the events has commenced. Go to the State Archives in Brisbane and look up the records for the Maryborough Base Hospital from May to June 1905. I am looking for the exact diagnosis and a possible medical explanation of the original source of infection. Check under Queensland State Health Department. See what references they have under pneumonic plague. Keep all inquiries low key and watch your accent. It will look damn strange for a Frenchman probing into such an odd subject. End.'

Cole sat on the end of the bed and opened the 'Plague' folder that Sue had given him. Near the top were newspaper articles from local newspapers relating to the deaths in Childers. These were dated from May 12, 1905. Chappie walked in carrying freshly laundered khaki uniforms on wire hangers and hung them in the wardrobe.

'Chappie, pull up a chair and listen to this.'
Cole read out the newspaper reports.

'May 12, 1905. A case of supposed plague was reported by the Health Officer, Doctor Challands to the Chairman of the Isis Shire Council, the patient being now isolated at the Isis district hospital. Mr. Martin, M.L.A., still continues in an

exceedingly low condition.'

'May 15, The serum taken by the health officer from a suspected plague patient (an Italian named Gardoni) and forwarded to Doctor Ham for examination proves the case to be true plague. A trained nurse and a special doctor will come by the Brisbane train tomorrow (Monday), for the purpose of taking charge of the case. An inspector is also coming.'

*'May 17, Doctor Baxter-Tyrie, representing the Health Commissioner, arrived last night with a trained nurse. The nuisance inspector took the plague case over to-day. The doctor did not expect that the patient would live, but **there is little or no likelihood of further cases cropping up**.'*

He placed heavy emphasis on the last line.

'May 17. The Mayor said that plague had again broken out close to Maryborough. Alderman McGhie asked what the Council was doing with reference to the extermination of rats. The mayor replied that this matter was not in the hands of the Council but the Government medical officer had a man engaged in laying poison.'

*'May 19. Though the patient Gardoni succumbed to the dreaded malady yesterday evening Doctor Baxter-Tyrie assures the public that there is **little or no likelihood of any further cases cropping up.'***

'May 22. Speaking to Doctor Baxter-Tyrie, of the Health Department, (says the Isis "Recorder"), he informed us that whilst there is not the slightest doubt that the general cleaning up throughout the town of Childers discovered a number of plague-infected rats, serious alarm by on the part of the public would not be justified by the circumstance.

It is extremely probable that the disease was introduced

here by a plague rat from some infected centre and the
animal then communicated the disease to the native rodents,
numbers of which have been dying around the town and its
environs for some months past. So virulent indeed has the
disease been that it has practically exterminated the vermin.
The doctor assured us there is no earthly reason for a
scare.'

Chappie stood up and stretched, 'Hey Cole, that Doctor Baxter-Tyrie bloke seemed pretty casual about an outbreak of the Black Plague.'

Cole thought for a moment before he answered, 'Yes, extremely casual for a government inspector. Throughout history and in every culture the presence of plague was publicly announced, and the population controlled to prevent an epidemic. This is the first time I have heard of government guys playing it down. There has got to be an underlying reason.'

Chappie picked up the newspaper articles Cole had just read and one by one neatly filed them away as he asked, 'Yea, well all these articles explain the Childer's outbreak of Bubonic Plague but why did the Maryborough episode start with a primary infection of the pneumonic strain?'

'It would please Sue if we found that out before we leave.'

'Are you gonna tell her what we're doing here?' Quizzed Chappie.

'Lord no!' Cole answered quickly. 'She will find out soon enough and I am quite sure she is going to be very, very angry. So, let's just face that tiger when we get to it.'

DAY TWO – A Vicious Seizure

MAY 25, 3.45am, 1905.

"That the star-gazers, having writ on death,

May say, the plague is banish'd by thy breath."

Shakespeare, *Venus and Adonis (1593)*

'Mrs. Edwards, please, please wake up. Mrs. Edwards? It's Kate, Kate O'Connell.' Her loud and insistent thumping on the front door was impossible for anyone to ignore.

'Oh God, O God, I think John is dying. I don't know what else to do. Mrs. Edwards, can you hear me?'

As the front door opened the kindly Letitia Edwards was silhouetted by the pale-yellow lamplight. Standing before her was a tall, thin girl with an elfin face wearing a dirty white nightdress. She was trembling in the crisp morning breeze, brushing at wayward brown curls that kept blowing across her mouth.

'Kate, dear, it's 3.30 in the morning, what has happened?'

'I'm so sorry Mrs. Edwards but it's John, he's been ill for days and now I think he's dying. We can't afford a doctor to come. Doctor Robinson, the Health Officer, came around yesterday afternoon but there wasn't much he could do. And now, now I think he's dying. Will you come, please?'

'Certainly, dear, but you must first come inside.'

As they walked into the house Arthur Edwards passed his wife a blanket. Mrs. Edwards draped it around Kate's shoulders, 'Here Kate wrap this around you while I get decent. 'Arthur, would you get Kate a cup of tea dear.'

Kate pulled at her fingers in frustration, 'Mrs. Edwards, please, John needs us.'

Arthur placed a comforting hand on Kate's arm and said in his stoic, matter-of-fact voice, 'Your brother needs you to keep well Kate. Get warm and drink your tea. Lettie is not one to dawdle.'

Kate encompassed the warm cup in her cold fingers and sipped gratefully. In a short span of time Letitia was back down the hallway pulling on her jacket, 'Come dear, I'll see what can be done.'

Bracing against the night air the middle-aged woman and the young girl hurried across the dirt track of Pallas Street to the decaying home of Richard O'Connell and his seven motherless children.

So sad, thought Letitia as she approached the rotting front door. Even this wooden shack had a picturesque quality when their mother was alive. She managed to keep it neat and clean, though only the Lord knows how with so many young ones. After heavy rain the tiny front yard was littered with pink blooms of local wildflowers. It was almost homely.

More O'Connell children were waiting for Kate to return. Ten-year-old Richard junior and nine-year-old May swung open the door as soon as Mrs. Edwards and their eldest sister approached. Fifteen-year-old James was sitting cross-legged on the soiled wooden floor cradling the head of his ill brother. Seven-year-old Ellen was sitting next to John clinging to his emaciated arm.

James looked up and pushed his matted auburn hair out of his eyes with a blood splattered hand. Mrs. Edwards gave a start at the dreadful change in the child. His handsome face was pasty white with shadows ringing his bright, inquisitive eyes now sunken from exhaustion and malnutrition. This lovable young rogue was just learning the power of his pleasing looks. Letitia had heard quite a few stories where James' easy smile and charisma had regularly charmed store owners into giving him food and sometimes even the odd lolly. Now he was speaking dully as if the effort of talking was sapping the last of his energy, 'Mrs. Edwards, John's hot and coughs a lot. What can we do?' He looked down at his brother and continued wiping John's blood-stained mouth with a grey cloth that he rinsed in a bowl of crimson water.

'Poor child, you're ready to collapse. Lie down and rest for a while. I'll tend to your brother.'

Reluctantly he relinquished his place and allowed Mrs. Edwards to cradle his brother's head. On his hands and knees, he crawled to the closest wall and lent against it shutting his eyes. Ellen lay down next to her ill brother and placed her arm protectively over him. She was the wild one; game for anything from the time she could walk. Her mass of flaxen, wiry curls almost reached her waist because she permitted no one to cut them. But for all her wild ways she had a loving nature, bringing home any hurt or hungry creature she might find. A lump was forming in Letitia's throat as she watched the little girl try desperately to comfort her dying brother.

'It will be alright now, John, Mrs. Edwards is here to help you.'

John's breathing was labored, and his chest rattled loudly with each precious breath. Letitia stroked his brow and crooned soothing words. Ellen patted his hand. Without warning a violent coughing outburst sprayed blood-filled sputum over the floor, down Mrs. Edward's dress and all over Ellen, as the young man's body spasmed. He twisted and writhed, gasping frantically to force some air into his lungs. Rolling backwards and forwards he sent Ellen flying across the room where she remained huddled terrified in the corner until the spasm ended. His energy spent John lay on his back with eyes glazed staring at the black shadows on the ceiling. His chest still heaved laboriously fighting for air.

Kate and Richard stood by helplessly wanting to do something but not knowing how they could be useful. Nine-year-old May remained sitting in the darkest corner of the single room cottage trying to block out the horror by rocking backwards and forwards with her hands over her ears humming tunelessly while a listless grey kitten lay on her lap. Three-year-old Johanna began to cry, which at least gave Richard something to do.

'Here Jo catch this. Catch it.' He wiggled a piece of paper in front of her, playfully snatching it away as she reached out a boney hand to take it.

Kate picked up a rusty bucket, 'I'll get more water, Mrs. Edwards.' She headed outside towards the corroded water tank. As the bucket slowly filled, she looked skywards at the first fingers of sunlight.

But an ominous rattle from inside the house broke the dewy peace. Kate collected the bucket and rushed inside to see blood spewing from John's mouth, heave after torturous heave. Mrs. Edwards was holding him firmly by the shoulders. In a vicious seizure the last of John's life-giving breath was expelled from his tortured chest and no amount of thrashing and gasping would allow air to flow back in. He rocked from side to side as his life ebbed away. Cradling in Mrs. Edward's arms finally John lay still. His suffering ended.

May smiled in relief and put a grubby finger to her lips as Kate walked in through the door, 'Don't wake up, John.'

Mrs. Edwards looked up at Kate and shook her head. Without a word Kate placed the bucket near the door and walked over to take May by the hand, 'Come with me, May.'

'But John's asleep. He might need something when he wakes up.'

'Mrs. Edwards will look after him. May, please come now, just for a little while. You need some air.'

'You will call out Mrs. Edwards if you need me.'

'I promise, May.'

May nodded and went with Kate. They were surprised to meet their neighbour, Matilda Schafer, bustling up the road. She was the tallest woman the children had seen in their short lives. Matilda was a middle-aged spinster woman with no children of her own but an enormous capacity for nurturing. Anyone ill that came across her path could depend on receiving her tender attention.

'Oh, Kate dear, what has happened? My brother Bill just arrived home from work at the wharves. He said he saw you and Lettie rushing towards your house. Is it John? Is he all right?'

Kate shook her head from side to side just a little so that May would not see.

'That is very kind, Miss Schafer. Mrs. Edwards is with John now. I must take May for a walk.'

'I understand dear. I'll help Lettie with the preparations.'

'There's a bucket of clean water inside the door. Thank you, Miss Schafer. I have to go to work soon or there'll be no money for this week's rent, especially with John . . ."

She stopped short, not wanting her sister to know John was dead in such a callous manner. May tugged impatiently at Kate's grubby skirt, 'What do we have to talk about, Kate and where are we walking to?'

'Come with me now and you'll find out.'

Matilda Schafer strode into the room where Ellen was still holding her dead brother's hand.

'Tilly dear, it's only just dawn. How did you know?'

'Bill saw you crossing the road with Kate so we knew it would be some type of emergency. We'd best get started with the preparations.'

Ellen's head flicked up, her eyes full of tears and concern.

'What do you mean preparations? What are you going to do to John?'

'My lamb, look at him. He can't stand at the pearly gates like that. We have to wash him and comb his hair, just like when you used to go to Sunday school.'

'Mother made us put on clean clothes as well.'

'Does John have another set of clothes?'

Ellen shook her head, 'Ah well, no matter. Now you go with James and help look after Johanna. There's a good girl.'

As the children filed outside Matilda turned to attend to the boy, but Letitia was now standing between her friend and the dead boy. 'Lettie, what is the matter? I've come to help you prepare the boy for a Christian burial.'

'Tilly, you did not see the way he died. God willing, it will not be something that spreads, but just in case, you will not touch him. Agreed?'

'Now really, Lettie, I am strong as an ox.'

But Letitia held her position. With a sigh Tilly gave into her friend.

'Alright, if it will ease your mind, dear. I've come to help not argue.'

After numerous buckets of water Letitia was satisfied that John and his clothing were as clean as they could make him.

'Lettie, where is the father?' asked Matilda.

Letitia nodded towards town, 'Still on the drink I suppose. Well, when he comes home, he'll need to plan a funeral.'

PRESENT DAY 2 - MAY 25.

Sue had been running late that morning. Cole utilized the time by collecting soil samples on the site of the old O'Connell hut. Meticulously he wrote in his notebook and on the sample's plastic bag the precise location of each collection point.

After filing them away in a metal suitcase secured in the boot of the red four-wheel drive, he poured himself a cup of coffee. Years of research in isolated places had taught him to carry a thermos of coffee. It was a habit he now maintained whenever he was working outside.

For a few quiet moments he could almost imagine the O'Connell's hut but the grey Holden roaring around the corner dissipated his thoughts. After thumping the driver's side door a few times, it finally opened and a flustered Sue jumped out, 'I am so sorry Mr. Leedon. Simon, my eldest, and his mates were caught smoking on the school grounds yesterday, so I had to see the headmaster today or else he'd be suspended. They said it would only take a few minutes, but he went on and on and on about it.' Sue drew in another agitated breath, 'Bloody hell, no wonder some of these guys get no respect from the kids. They just love to hear their own voices.'

Cole laughed which completely caught Sue off balance. He was always so formal and contained. But when his deep green eyes lit up in genuine pleasure, he was strikingly handsome, 'Coffee, Sue? Milk and sugar, right?'

Sue nodded, 'Oh God, a cup of coffee would be heaven right now.'

He handed her a cup still smiling and said, 'And just call me

Cole, please.'

'OK, sure. Now can I ask what was so funny?'

'Children and mothers are the same around the world. A few months ago, I was doing some research in a small Ituri village near the Democratic Republic of Congo. Two boys were caught playing in a waterhole instead of gathering food to contribute to the evening meal. The boys were dragged in front of the chief who was decked out in all his bones and feathers. After a great deal of chatter, he decreed that the boys would stand watch all night on an empty stomach. This he said would remind them that each villager had a responsibility to all the others.'

'So, what was so funny?'

'Oh, as the mothers walked away, they said exactly the same thing. That they could have been sitting in the shade doing some chores instead of having to listen to a man going on and on because he loved the sound of his own voice.'

'You could understand what they were saying?

'Over the years I have been in the area quite a bit. An ability to pick up the local language fast is a prerequisite for survival.'

'If you say so. Thanks for the coffee but we'd better get into it. I have to pick Josh up from swimming practice.'

'Sure thing, we were discussing how the first victim may have contracted the pneumonic strain of plague. You said that rumor pointed to the sacking from a Hong Kong freighter; any other suggestions?'

'Well, yes actually. Poverty was a way of life for those kids. They survived on handouts from their neighbours, and they were regularly seen around the wharves scrounging for food from the ships and going through the garbage at the rear of shops.' Sue wiped the sweat from her face. 'Cole, do you mind if we stand under that tree, I'm frying out here?' They walked towards a large tree near the intersection and Sue carried on with the story, 'Neighbours reported to the newspapers after the event that the children used the sewer as their playground.'

'A sewer! And where is that exactly.'

'There is a copy of an old Maryborough map in the folder I gave you, but it was filled in donkey's years ago. It ran from the west side of Kent Street to the east side then it continued under Adelaide Street. This was the enclosed part of the sewers. It was about ten feet high with cement walls and a roof with a flooring of stones and bricks. Locals said that the mud and ooze squelched up beneath the kid's feet. From there it was an open sewer that passed through Queen's Park alongside Lennox Street and emptied into the river. They said that at low tide it stank to the high heavens and the O'Connell children played in this sewer from morning till night.'

'So, no doubt it would have been an ideal habitat for rats. I have lived in many poverty-stricken countries where a fat rat was a very good dinner indeed. If the children were as hungry as all that they may have resorted to catching rats to eat in which case, they would need to skin them.'

'And how does this help?'

'John O'Connell just might have caught an infected rat. When he skinned it, he may have inhaled the bacterium directly into his lungs causing a primary infection. This would account for the disease outbreak only in its pneumonic form.'

Sue nodded as she wiped the trickles of sweat escaping from her armpit and brushed away the flies collecting in the corners of her eyes.

'Look that is enough for today, Sue. I will see you here tomorrow morning, ok?'

Even under the tree the air was hot and sticky, but Cole looked as immaculate as he did this morning. How the hell does he do that she thought as she trudged back to her car. She jerked open the door as Cole pulled up next to her.

'Sue do not worry too much about Simon. Young men must explore everything in the world that surrounds them.' He let out the clutch and was gone. He's such a strange man she thought as the slash of red disappeared towards town.

*

Chappie was lounging on the mini verandah outside the motel room studying Sue's plague folder when Cole returned. He noticed Cole was a little more animated than usual today.

'Chappie, we are getting somewhere now,' he slammed the car door. 'Get the team organized for a dig. There was a sewer near the O'Connell hut that might have been a breeding ground for plague rats. Push the paperwork through for a priority sample collection.'

'Sure thing, Cole, I'll get right on it, but you should read this.' He pointed to a newspaper article in Sue's file.

THE MARYBOROUGH CHRONICLE June 24, 1905. 'THE PLAGUE OUTBREAK: Who is to Blame? On the morning of the boy's death a neighbour, Mrs. Edwards, went across for an hour and a half in neighbourly sympathy. It is stated that a medical man in Maryborough diagnosed the boy 'Connell's case to be of plague; but the government medical officer considered the case one of pneumonia.'

Cole looked at Chappie, 'Well, well, so the conflict between the local doctors and the government started from the beginning. Why do you think? To stop public panic maybe; but how could they stop it from spreading if the people were not told?'

Chappie shook his head, 'I don't know but it is the most secretive case of plague we've ever come across. Right,' said Chappie as he stood up. 'I'll get that dig organised.'

DAY THREE – A Decomposing Corpse

MAY 26, 1905.

'. . . constrained by poverty, they stayed in their houses

where they sickened by thousands a day.'

Giovanni Boccaccio, *Decameron (1353)*

As Matilda Schafer walked up the path to the O'Connell door Richard O'Connell threw it open to block her entry and allowed the door to slam shut behind him, 'What do ya want now ya interfering old biddy?'

Matilda puffed herself up to full imposing height and crossed her arms firmly over her very ample bosom, 'Richard O'Connell, it's the children I've come to see, not you. So, you'll be kind enough to move aside.'

Richard's hands were shaking badly either from anger or alcoholism, she was not sure which, but either way Matilda was not one to be intimidated. She stood her ground as O'Connell screamed in her face, 'Don't ya think ya be telling me what ta do in my own home. Get away with ya and stick ya beak inta someone else's business.'

Matilda softened her approach just a little. Behind this shell of a man was the faintest image of the Richard she remembered when his wife was alive. Not a well-educated man and probably only capable of hard manual labor but he'd kept the same menial job for years and managed to pay the rent and feed his large family. 'I know tis a difficult time for you. Lettie laid out John for his funeral because a father shouldn't have to do that for his son. I'm here now to help the children in any way I can. Richard, you don't have to cope with this alone.'

'What soppy woman's talk ya drivelling. I don't need no help to look after me own. Get moving an keep away from me kids.'

Rather than risking the possibility of Richard taking out his anger on the children Matilda turned and walked back home to wait.

Later that day, while hanging out the washing on the backyard line, Matilda heard the clanging of the old ice truck bell as it trundled up her street.

'Lord, I almost forgot. Another day and we'd have nought but spoiled food to eat.'

As she rushed out, purse in hand, Matilda was just in time to see Richard O'Connell heading for town. Matilda offered a little prayer, 'What a blessing, thank you Lord for clearing the path.' She quickly filled the ice chest and arranged the food back inside it then decided to first pay a visit to Letitia. Her friend might have liked to see the children while Richard was away.

*

After a few short raps on her friend's front door Matilda was surprised to see that it was Arthur who opened it.

'My word Arthur, you gave me a start. Why aren't you at work? You sick?'

'Never a sick day in my life, Tilly. You know that.' With a twinkle in his eye he added, 'The devil looks after his own, eh?'

'Arthur Edwards, I truly cannot understand how our Lord allows you into his church.'

'I'll tell ya why, because Lettie makes me give a king's

ransom when the plate comes round. That's why.'

'What piffle you talk,' she smacked him on the arm and brushed passed him into the house. Arthur enjoyed being irreverent, particularly if he could shock his devoutly religious friend, Tilly Schafer. She knew he was joking, but sometimes he went too far, and it strained their friendship of many years. But he had the charm of the devil when he wanted, and he always managed to worm his way back into her good books.

'You've had your fun at my expense now I've no more time for idle banter. I spoke with Richard O'Connell. He was in the foulest mood. Would not let me see the children and ordered me off. Can you imagine the cheek?'

'T'is a sad state of affairs, over there. I'd feel easier if you an' Lettie would keep away. But I know I'd be wasting me breath to try and stop ya.'

'You thought well. They are God's children, and someone has to look out for them. Now where is Lettie? While Richard is out, we'll visit the children.'

'I've just got her off to sleep in fact. A little chicken soup and a strong cup of black tea, that'll fix most things. It's probably nought but a bad cold. She's got pain in her head an' stomach and all her joints are aching. Perhaps you could come back later when she's awake and feeling better.'

'Please give her my love and tell her I'll be back soon.'
Arthur watched Matilda Walk determinedly across the road. He knew from years of experience not to try and stop his wife or her friend from lending a hand to anyone who may need it. But he was uneasy this time. From what Kate had said her brother first became ill with the same symptoms Lettie was showing now. He'd better wait and see. She'd

skin him alive if he called the doctor out for nothing.

Matilda was now pushing open the door.

That's odd, thought Arthur, with all those children nobody let her in. With a shake of his head he shut the door and went to check on his wife.

*

As Matilda walked into the dimness of the single room hut her stomach wrenched at the overpowering stink. She swallowed hard several times to subside the churning. Never had she been one to go quietly through life, but standing on the edge of such poverty and soul-destroying muck she lowered her voice to a whisper, 'Children, are you there? It's so dark in here I can't see too well yet.'

'Miss Schafer, I am so glad you're here.'

'Ellen, is that you dear?' Carefully she picked her way over the unidentifiable piles of rotting mess. 'My goodness, how can any father allow his children to live like this? Tis a disgrace.' As her eyes became accustomed to the dark Matilda could see the children huddled in the shadowy corners clinging to each other for comfort. Her big heart melted, and she extended her long arms in readiness to encircle them all, 'Poor little lambs. It's so sad to lose a sibling.' She bustled towards them then stopped in gut-wrenching horror. It took a few heartbeats for the magnitude of the awfulness before her to fully register. There on the sacking bed, where he'd been left two days ago was the decomposing corpse of John O'Connell. 'Children, come with me, outside now, away from this.'

May started crying, 'No, no! We have to stay inside. You

know what father is like. He told us to stay here until he comes back.'

'But he allows you to roam the streets. He's not been bothered for years about where you were.'
This time it was James who reinforced his sister's fears.

'He's ashamed because he can't afford a funeral. No one is supposed to know.'
Matilda tilted his chin up to better see his face. It was strained and sallow.

'You're the man of the house now Jamie, but that doesn't mean you can't grieve. Stay here then if you must while I seek out Mr. Steadman. I believe this to be his area of authority.'

PRESENT DAY 3 - MAY 26.

'Sue, Sue. Just hold on a second. I must clarify something here. Why did Matilda Schafer need this Mr. Steadman instead of Doctor Crawford Robinson?'

'Doctor Robinson would only have called Mr. Steadman. It just saved time to contact Steadman first. The Department of Public Nuisance looked after any community and sanitation problems.'

Cole's mobile phone interrupted Sue's explanation. He answered it and abruptly walked a few steps away. Although he had his back to her Sue could still hear snippets of the conversation.

'. . . Sir . . . plague source . . . not that easy . . . country town. Suspicion . . . code five in place . . . parameters set.'

With the conversation finished he turned back to Sue, shutting off the phone. He seemed preoccupied and stood for a moment intently studying the horizon.

Sue followed his gaze. Against the morning glare she could just make out a dark outline, 'Wow, that's odd,' Sue said as she shaded her eyes for a better view. 'We don't usually have helicopters flying around town.' She looked at Cole suspiciously. 'Funny, you seemed to know it was there.'

'I could hear it. Once you have lived in war-ravaged countries you become sensitive to noises like the distant drone of helicopter rotors.'

'Yea? Well, I supposed you would.' Unconvinced Sue turned her attention back to the helicopter.

'Strange, it seems to be circling the area that was cordoned off this morning. We were just talking about it yesterday, you know, the Kent Street, Adelaide Street section where the old sewer used to run. They seem to be digging it up or something.'

'Sue, I am afraid we must finish up now. I have been called away and school is nearly out anyway.'

'Cole, how do you know it's a half day at school today?'

'You must have mentioned it, or I heard someone talking. It is not important now but where shall we meet tomorrow?'

'Ah, now, tomorrow they have what they call a Ghost Tour. My boys are staying with friends on a cane farm, so I've booked you and I in for the tour. A bus will pick us up in front of City Hall in the early evening, so we'll have plenty of time to reconstruct day four's events before it's time to leave. Oh, and dinner is included in the tour.'

'Sue I really do appreciate the trouble you have gone to but why would I be interested in a Ghost Tour?'

'Because it's really a historic tour and they focus a great deal on the plague victims. They take you for a walk through the cemetery and you can actually stand next to the graves of all the people you are researching; the O'Connell children, Mrs. Edwards, Nurse Bauer, Nurse Wiles.'

'They take you to the grave sites?'

'Yes, and walk through the wharf area. Some of the pubs and official buildings from 1905 are still standing. I thought it might be of help to you.'

'This might save an awful lot of time. Yes, thank you Sue,

'OK. We'll meet in front of the City Hall 5.15pm.' He gave a sharp, preoccupied nod and left.

'What's his problem?' Sue asked herself. 'Talk about man-moods he's like two people sometimes. Ah, well, better pick the boys up from school.'

*

On his way back to this motel room Cole made a detour past Kent Street. He maneuvered his car around the roadblock and parked under a large leafy tree next to an unmarked caravan. A pool of water was forming in the dust from the overworked air-conditioner. Chappie finished his conversation with two tall, fair haired women in white coats. They quickly retreated back into the chilled interior of the caravan. One greeted Cole with a quick nod and a terse,

'Guten Tag (good day).'
While the other commented,

'Es ist heiß (it's hot),' and slammed the door shut behind her.

'Any problems, Chappie?'
'Not so far. Our paperwork was accepted, the relative authorities have been obliging. Our German experts in there,' he nodded towards the caravan, 'have been collecting soil samples from the old sewer.'

'Did you need to dig up much area?'
'Hardly any at all really. Once the backhoe had dug down deep enough those two used some gismo they bought with them to bore horizontally into the dirt. They can tell if they are following the bottom layer of the sewer because sensors on its tip relay the soil components back to their computer.'

'Ah, German engineering is hard to beat,' admired Cole. 'Before I go, please come to my car for a minute, Chappie, I want to show you something.'

Chappie and Cole jumped in the front seats. Cole reached over to the back seat, flipped the lid of a black briefcase and dragged out some papers all in one swift movement.

'Here, what do you make of these?' Cole handed Chappie a newspaper article.

THE MARYBOROUGH CHRONICLE June 24, 1905. THE PLAGUE OUTBREAK. 'Who is to Blame? It appears that the eldest boy of the O'Connell family 'the first case' died under circumstances sufficient to have aroused suspicion that his complaint was something very unusual. The body turned black rapidly and decomposing was allowed to lie in the house for thirty-six hours, while the other motherless children were living in the same house.'

Chappie nodded, 'Alright, the first death was in May, and this is dated June. So, a month later it became public knowledge that John's body had turned black the most visual indicator that plague is about.'

'It is so strange that nobody appeared to voice publicly their suspicion that it might be plague. For a contrast read this article about an outbreak in Sydney.'

The Deadly Disease – The Black Death in Australia. Arthur Payne, 33, a wharfie in Sydney was diagnosed with having bubonic plague on January 20, 1900. Payne lived in the close-knit community of The Rocks. The policeman posted at the door generated immediately interest. Payne was collected by ambulance and taken to the Quarantine Station at North Head. Within days others in The Rocks area began to fall ill. Sir William Lyne, the NSW premier quarantined the area; no one except health inspectors and cleaners who had been inoculated against the contagion was allowed to leave or enter.

Citizens were given the choice of staying in their homes or moving to the Quarantine Station. The State member for the area, Billy Hughes, pointed out to the Premier that

many of The Rocks inhabitants worked outside the area.
If they could not leave they would starve. He agreed to pay
bona fida residents of the quarantined area six shillings a
day for the duration. When word of this got out the area
was besieged with the town's homeless attempting to
become bona fide residents.

The Rocks area was one of the oldest and poorest in
Sydney. Houses were badly maintained and lacked
sanitation. It was an ideal breeding ground for rats. An
architect, George McCredie, was bought in to oversee the
clearing or whitewashing of the slums. When floorboards
were torn up, the bloated carcasses of plague killed rats
were revealed. His authoritarian purge resulted in
hundreds of homes being demolished and belongings ruined
with whitewash and disinfectant. Accusations of indignities
and invasion of privacy poured into the office of Billy
Hughes.'

Chappie finished reading and handed the paper back to
Cole, 'I would say that one of two things occurred here.
Either they were being unusually cautious before declaring
plague or the authorities had a reason to keep it quiet.'

'I have to agree, Chappie. I will head back to the motel
while you tie up any loose ends. You had better get the
caravan out of here before someone asks too many
questions.

'Righto, I'll be back by sixteen hundred hours.'

DAY FOUR - Diligence

MAY 27, 1905.

'Ring-around-a-rosie, a pocket full of posies,

ashes, ashes, We all fall down.'

Popular nursery rhyme (1790's)

His Worship, Mayor William Dawson was an imposing figure of a man who carried the responsibility of his station with ease upon his broad shoulders. Usually, the most amiable of men he was at present showing signs of extreme concern. His plumb cheeks were florid, and he continually stroked his long steel grey beard while reading out loud to Doctor Crawford Robinson, 'The following is the report written by Mr. G.D. Steadman, the Inspector of Nuisances, after he was called out to the home of Richard O'Connell by Miss Matilda Schafer.

"The premises, through lack of attention and household necessaries, were in a filthy condition. The floorboards were saturated with sputum and other excretions of the children. You may imagine the state of the boy's bed of rough bags. These bags had been taken to the O'Connell home after being discarded by a freighter from Hong Kong. The father had put them to use as bedding for his children. The Health Department has been contacted and a burial arranged."

'What do you say, Doctor Robertson, is there a connection to deaths in Childers? Do we have plague in Maryborough as well as an epidemic of Dengue Fever?"

'Mayor Dawson from my observations of the child, John O'Connell, his symptoms were similar to Dengue hemorrhagic fever in the last stages. If you take into consideration the living conditions of the child it could well have been that he was suffering from a number of diseases that, when combined, may have caused his death.'

Mayor Dawson slammed his fist onto the desktop, 'Do not dance with me, Robinson. You are here now because I know you have not signed the death certificate. At any moment now Doctor Lee Garde is going to stalk in here and put me through the mill. You know eradicating plague in Queensland has been his soapbox for years. And in full steam behind him will be that firebrand Doctor Henry Croker Garde.'

Doctor Crawford Robinson replied calmly, 'As the Superintendent of the Maryborough General Hospital, Doctor Lee Garde has to remain diligent for plague outbreaks and as the resident surgeon at that hospital Doctor H. C. Garde would be lax in his duties if he did not act on any suspicion of plague.'

'Diligent? Lee is a bloodhound. He just will not let go. If he suspects we have had a case of plague he will be baying at the Health Department day and night until they pay to clean out the rats just like he did in Toowoomba.'

'Mayor, you say that as if you are opposed to rat eradication program.'

'All I am saying is that he did not make many friends in the Health Department with his incessant demands. Maryborough does not need an over-zealous doctor stirring up trouble, particularly not now!'

'Why is now any different to any other time when people's lives are at stake?'

'Good God, open your eyes, Robinson. Are you aware

that the President of the New South Wales Board of Health, Doctor Ashburton Thompson, will be in Brisbane on June six?'

'I do not understand what he has to do with this case.'

'Then let me give you the details. You do know that because of plague in Queensland the New South Wales government has placed an embargo on all of our produce. So, nothing can be sold over the border.'

'Yes, of course. It has added more hardship to the lives of many of my patients.'

'Then you need to be aware that in June Doctor Ashburton Thompson is meeting with Doctor Burnett Ham, who you know is the Queensland Commissioner of Public Health, to discuss the removal of those plague restrictions. That Childers episode almost halted the negotiations. Doctor Baxter-Tyrie got the situation under control.'

Doctor Crawford was horrified, 'Sir, you cannot call that under control, it was a state government cover up surely.'

'No! It was a government contingency plan activated to save the livelihood of thousands of Queenslanders and Childers has had no more outbreaks. If we have a case of plague here it could mean the end of any discussions for years. If you put plague on the death certificate it will be there for public viewing forevermore. Are you certain it was plague that killed John O'Connell?'

'Well, Mayor, I cannot say in all honesty that I am certain. Under the circumstances I could be within my rights to sign the cause of death as Dengue Fever, Bronchopneumonia and Syncope.'

'Thank you, Crawford. Let us hope that there are no more deaths of this nature.'

PRESENT DAY 4 - MAY 27.

By the time the Silverline bus pulled up in front of City Hall Cole was leaning against a street pole, his legs casually crossed. His spectacular trademark boots caught the attention of everyone sitting in a window seat.

As the bus doors opened he pushed himself off the pole and followed Sue to their seats in the front row. Catching a glimpse of those boots in the mirror, the bus driver turned around for a better look which caused many of the passengers to strain their necks forward or half stand up to follow his gaze. Sue caught his eye with a venomous look and 'Ted' as his name badge announced returned to his duties.

'I think you enjoy being noticed, Cole.'

'In my profession, Sue, it could be a matter of life and death. These boots draw attention. They are so distinctive that most people remember what they looked like.'

'And how would remembering your boots save your life here?'

'Not so much here but in places like the Republic of Congo, for example, western aid workers, doctors and peacekeepers disappear frequently. Wearing something distinctive makes it easier to trace the final movements of a missing team member. Some wear heavy silver jewelry, some have unique tattoos, others may have facial piercings. I opted for the boots.'

Ted's voice came over the speaker, 'This is our first stop ladies and gentlemen. Rose Hill was built in 1865 and is reported to have a number of ghosts. We will be having the first course of our progressive dinner on the verandah overlooking the magnificent grounds.

Afterwards we'll have a tour of the house which is full of antiques from the period, and where you might just run into one of the resident ghosts. Enjoy.'

*

Back in the motel room Chappie was on the phone to Lurman, the French team member who had now stationed himself in Brisbane.

'Ello, Chappie, can you 'ear me clearly?'

'Clear as crystal, Lurman, go ahead.'

'First thing in the morning I 'vill be in the Queensland State Archives. I check for records on cases of pneumonic plague. Perhaps such files will be in the Health Department records.'

'Yea, well good bloody luck. I've got the death certificate for John O'Connell in front of me. Doctor Crawford signed it stating cause of death to be 'Dengue Fever Bronchopneumonia Syncope.'

'Ah, you 'ave the certificates of the death for the victims. Bon, bon, it is a good start. When the time permits I vill visit the Queensland Maritime Museum. It is a possibility I might find a name for the mysterious ship from Hong Kong that was suspected of carrying this plague to Maryborough. But tonight, I find a good French restaurant and once again sample the tastes of home.'

'Too rich for my tastes but live it up. Cole's gonna be in contact 1700 hours tomorrow.'

'Bon. Lurman out.'

Chappie went back to his fish and chips as he studied the latest reports from France and the Republic of Congo. In Montpellier, France, Cole was head of a team working with archeologists excavating a mass grave from the 14th century full of plague victims. It was their job to search for usable DNA tissue. Over one third of the world's population had been decimated by the plague outbreak when these people had died. It had activated for no obvious reason and swept unabated across borders and oceans with equal ease. After three potent years of changing the course of nations, wars, and families it spluttered and fell dormant.

It had flared up again in its deadliest form of pneumonic plague in the deepest heart of the Congo Republic. Cole had to split his main team of doctors and plague researchers into three.   One was in France collecting ancient and often deteriorated plague DNA. One had been sent to the Zobia diamond mine in the Democratic Republic of Congo. One was now in Maryborough, Queensland, Australia studying the conditions leading up to this outbreak.

Their mission was to determine why the disease had suddenly activated in its pneumonic form without the precursor of a bubonic outbreak. At the moment thousands of lives were at risk every day but if it spread into the densely populated cities, it would be impossible to control.

*

In a flurry of dust, the bus slowed to a halt in front of the Maryborough Cemetery. Cole and Sue stepped down to be faced with a theatrical coffin filled with torches. With the marble tombstones as a backdrop half hidden by thick layers of dark leaves the tour host was most convincing in his undertaker's tall black hat and long coat.   He was accompanied by two 'grieving' widows in black crinolines and full widow's weeds. In a suitably sonorous voice, the undertaker instructed his charges to follow him around the tombstones.

In the distance a lamp was glowing and a young girl in a pink gingham dress and lacy bloomers was skipping in circles singing 'Ring-a-round a Rosie.' As the tour approached, she disappeared, and the undertaker stopped in front of a small memorial stone to address the group, 'Gather around please everybody so those at the back may hear my story. In 1905 the dreaded Black Plague visited our town and took as its first victim seventeen-year-old John O'Connell. In a matter of days all but two of his brothers and sisters would be struck dead by the same disease. They are buried here in pauper's graves.

You heard our ghostly aspiration singing the nursery rhyme 'Ring-a-round-a-rosie.' There is a school of thought which considers this child's song to be based on the Black Death epidemic which killed over twenty-five million people in the fourteenth century. The ring around a rosie, they say, refers to the round, red rash that is the first symptom of the disease. "A pocket full of posies" is the practice of carrying flowers and placing them around the infected person for protection. "Ashes" is a corruption or imitation of the sneezing sounds made by the infected person. Finally, "we all fall down" describes the many, many dead that often result from an outbreak of this disease. Now follow me please and keep together.'

As the tour moved towards the next glowing light Cole and Sue stepped closer to the white memorial stone embedded within it a plaque.

Cole read softly, 'Erected by the Maryborough City Council in memory of the O'Connell family. So, no individual headstones for these little ones.'

'No, the children's graves were only marked with numbers. At least now their lives are acknowledged.'

Cole studied the line of numbers that represented the children's graves. He wrote the numbers down so slowly in his notebook that Sue was forced to ask, 'Cole, what's the matter?'

'Sorry. It just makes you wonder. Why were they born only to die in such horrific pain surrounded by strangers?'

Cole turned to face her and for a fleeting moment the lantern light revealed, what? Vulnerability, regret? He was facing her, but his thoughts were elsewhere. What occupied him so intently she wondered? 'Cole we are going to the grave of Nurse Cecelia Bauer now. Cole?'

'Ah, yes, yes. Cecelia Bauer. I read up on your notes. Died on June six, 1905, the same day the outbreak was confirmed as pneumonic plague. She was twenty-two years old. She was on leave from the hospital preparing for her wedding in six weeks. Doctor Lee Garde called her back to help Nurse Wiles care for the O'Connell children. She was the second last person to die from pneumonic plague in this episode.'

They walked to the green tiled grave of Cecelia Bauer with its beautifully ornate headstone of the purest while marble. Their tour guide's resonant voice was crystal clear even from a distance, 'This headstone is actually the second to have been shipped out from Italy by Miss Bauer's fiancé, William Hastings, at enormous expense. After its six-week sea voyage the first marble slab was cracked so Mr. Hastings ordered another one, the one we see here today.'

One of the 'widows' in mourning regalia, complete with a full crinoline and black lace veil, stepped forward to deliver the next speech, 'Nurse Cecelia Bauer had been described as gentle, patient, sympathetic to suffering and alert in danger. She rejected the pleadings of her family and returned to nurse the dying O'Connell children. Very shortly she exhibited signs of contracting this terrible disease herself. Resigned to her fate she packed her belongings in four neat packages, one marked for each of her sisters and left them outside the ward door. Pneumonic plague was confirmed on the day of Cecelia Bauer's death.'

A shrouded hush momentarily descended on the audience before they were prompted to move again towards another section of the cemetery. Before following them, Cole studied the delicate carving on Cecelia's headstone and mused, 'Money can sometimes reflect the depth of someone's love, like this flawless piece of marble. But do you think O'Connell loved his children any less because he had no money? Was he a drunk because his wife had died, and he just could not cope?'

'I don't know Cole. There's not much light here. We'd better catch up before we trip over something. They are heading to the grave of Adelaide Wiles.'

'Ah, yes, the other nurse who helped care for the plague victims.'

'That's right. Nurse Bauer and Wiles knew that whatever the disease was so far had a one hundred percent death rate. They were not prepared to risk the lives of other nurses. So, they remained locked in their ward, refusing all assistance. Adelaide cared for Rose until she died knowing that she was soon to suffer the same end.'

Sue grabbed Cole's sleeve and pulled him back gently, 'Try and watch where you walk. There's a very low fence around the grave next to the 'Wiles plot. It's about ankle high, quite rusty but very dangerous for the unwary.'

Cole bent down and shone his torch on the tiny iron fence. Each ornate knob that surrounded the grave was topped with an extremely sharp five-pointed star, 'Glad you pointed that out Sue. It could make a mess of an ankle bone.'

Carefully Sue guided Cole around the protected grave until they stood with the tour group next to the Wiles family plot. A white headstone, taller than a man and exquisitely carved, stood in the center of the three-person grave site.

A small wall of painted white cement contained the layer of snowy white pebbles which now covered the graves.

The undertaker took his spot respectfully outside the low cement wall and began his speech, 'We are standing before the grave of Nurse Adelaide Wiles at the age of twenty-eight years old she was the last victim to be claimed by the pneumonic plague outbreak of 1905. Nurse Wiles was at the hospital when the O'Connell children arrived. She volunteered to look after them. In quick succession the children expired, and it was her sad duty to do the best she could to comfort her friend Cecelia Bauer until she too died. Adelaide herself passed away six days later. Now, ladies and gentlemen, for some truly bizarre crossings-over from this mortal world please follow the 'widows' and myself to the Scottish section.'

At these words the group burst into life again and chatted happily as they followed the undertaker's tall hat and the widows' sweeping gowns in a twisting trail around blackening headstones and broken monuments.

Sue stopped and signaled to Cole to follow her. They weaved their way to a monolithic obelisk of snowy white marble eerily shrouded in a faint blue glow from a small tour lantern placed at its base. Bold, black letters on its side announced the occupant to be Doctor Henry Croker Garde. Sue waited for the chattering group to move closer to the lilting notes of ghostly bagpipes which heralded the next story. She gave the impressive marble a few pats and said,

'Here we have Doctor Henry Croker Garde and his youngest daughter Eileen who tragically died in 1902 at only four years old. He was a fiery, brave, short-tempered but highly respected Dublin trained doctor. He was the resident surgeon at the Maryborough Hospital and was in the center of the mudslinging between the Queensland Health Department and the hospital after the last death from pneumonic plague.'

Cole was taking notes with his fancy penlight, 'What was Doctor Garde's medical background?'

'Just one thing Cole. When talking about this bloke we always call him H.C. Garde.'

'The reason being?'

'There were two Doctor Gardes at the Maryborough Hospital at the time. Henry Croker or H.C. as he was often called and his half nephew, Doctor Henry Lee Garde, who was the Medical Superintendent responsible for the whole hospital.'

'I can see how this would be confusing,' said Cole.

'Not only that,' continued Sue. 'But both men were from Ireland, and both served on the Maryborough Council as well as working at the Maryborough Hospital.'

'Yes, for historians that would be a nightmare. Do you have details on H.C.'s background?

'Sure, H.C. was born in Cork, Ireland, into a medical family. His grandfather, Doctor Abraham Colles, was world famous for a new bone fracture treatment he had devised. H.C. qualified as a Fellow of the Royal College of Physicians Ireland. He traveled as a ship's doctor and received a medal for bravery at sea by saving someone from drowning. He received another bravery award later on in his life. Eventually he set up private practice in Maryborough. He then did a stint as the Maryborough representative in state parliament, when he lost the next election, he returned here as the resident surgeon.'

'You called him 'fiery' why?'

'He was not a diplomatic man when it came to any work which he perceived to be slovenly by nursing staff. He had verbally abused a previous matron for being drunk on the job. He was also accused of threatening a nurse with a red-hot cauterizing iron for being too slow in theatre.'

'Not a man to be easily silenced then,' Cole thought he would have liked this man had they the chance to meet.

A lantern glow was moving around the headstones towards Cole and Sue.

'The tour!' cried Sue. 'I'll bet it's finished. They're probably looking for us.'

Just then the young girl in the pink gingham dress and lacy bloomers emerged from the darkness, 'Daddy says we have to go now.' She picked up the lantern at the base of the obelisk and turned it off. Holding her own lantern high she instructed, 'Please follow me carefully,' she skipped along the winding pathway back to the bus.

'Sue, before we get back to the bus where do we meet tomorrow?'

'Meet me at the O'Connell site and I'll take it from there.'

'And Sue, thanks for arranging this tonight. It has been more help that I can tell you.'

Next to the theatrical coffin the widows were fussing and waving for Cole and Sue to hurry. They dropped their borrowed torches into the coffin's belly and jumped on board.

DAY FIVE – Hoodlum Behaviour

MAY 28, 1905.

'The condition of the (plague) people was pitiable to

behold. They sickened by the thousands daily and

died unattended and without help.'

Giovanni Boccaccio, *Decamero* (1353).

'Doctor Robinson, one moment please.' Doctor Crawford Robinson stopped on the footpath in front of the O'Connell home. Doctor Graham Dixon hurried towards him from the Edward's home directly across the street, 'Ah, Crawford just the man I wanted to see.'

'Graham, I'm afraid I cannot indulge in casual conversation just at the minute. I have some very ill children to attend.'

'More O'Connell children, with the same symptoms?' Doctor Crawford Robinson nodded.

'Then I believe we have a serious problem. I have just attended Mrs. Letitia Edwards.'

'The neighbour who was with John O'Connell when he died?'

Doctor Graham Dixon took a step forward and dropped his voice, 'She is desperately ill with the same symptoms the O'Connell boy had before he died and now you say the other children are ill. I do not believe we are dealing with Dengue Fever here hemorrhagic or otherwise.'

Doctor Robinson's back stiffened and he began to fidget with a thread on his buttonhole as Doctor Graham Dixon continued with his suspicions, 'I fear we may be dealing with a form of plague. I know at the time you considered the cause of death to be Dengue Hemorrhagic Fever because this forms large patches of blood to accumulate under the skin. You know what I am leading to, Crawford. Plague is called Black Death because the blood accumulates under the skin and turns dark after death. This makes the skin of the corpse look black. Please think carefully Crawford; when you saw John O'Connell's body in the morgue had the skin darkened unnaturally?'

After his recent talk with the Mayor, Doctor Crawford Robinson did not wish to idly discuss the possibility of plague in the town. His speech became evasive and stilted,

'The corpse was in an advanced state of decomposition. It had lain in this house for thirty-six hours. At no time alive or dead did John O'Connell exhibit signs of bubonic plague. That is all that could be said on the matter.'

Doctor Graham Dixon studied his colleague's face closely,

'Crawford, Mrs. Edwards will probably die, and John's siblings are very ill, all within a few days of having contact with the first victim. Even the fatal strain of Dengue Fever does not spread that quickly. If we have plague, it must be reported to the mayor.'

'I agree, Graham. I have a meeting with the mayor this afternoon. I will pass on our suspicions. But for God's sake do not discuss this with anyone. You do not understand what is at stake.'

Doctor Dixon was taken aback at this unexpected statement, 'People's lives are at stake, isn't that enough?'

'Of course, I am only saying we must be sure it is plague before we incite public panic. Now I must attend to these children. Good day.'

*

Matilda Schafer opened the door and tried to usher a reluctant Doctor Crawford Robinson into the O'Connell cottage, 'Thank you for seeing the children today, Doctor. They are so desperately sick.'

Doctor Crawford Robinson planted himself just inside the doorway and announced coolly, 'Your brother, Miss Schafer, was most insistent, and stubborn. He hammered on my front door all the way through my breakfast.'

'Well, I did tell him it was urgent.'

'You condone his actions? I am shocked, Miss Schafer. Such hoodlum behavior is totally unnecessary. I had already assured him I would come here immediately I had finished my breakfast. Why I even had my neighbours peeking through their curtains to find the cause of the commotion.'

Matilda crossed her arms and took a deep breath, 'Doctor Robinson, my brother has the mildest of natures until he sees someone suffering and then he's as stubborn as a mule if he can do something about it.'

She started to walk into the room as she sniffed, 'These children are in a great deal of pain. You can consider yourself lucky that Bill only banged on your door.'

'Well, really! Miss Schafer, I am a doctor, not a bullyboy wharfie. I will not tolerate intimidation tactics.'

Doctor Crawford Robinson was quite startled by Matilda's attitude. He was usually spoken to in grateful reverent tones. Now he was being chided for finishing his breakfast when he never knew how long it would be before he had time to eat again, if it turned out to be a busy day.

'Then get to your doctoring and see what's wrong with these kiddies,' snapped Matilda.

'What are the symptoms?' asked the doctor tersely.

'It started with a headache and fever, then terrible bad pain in the stomach and around the heart with violent vomiting and a nagging cough.'

'I see. Their brother John had similar symptoms. How many are ill now and what are their ages?'

'Fifteen-year-old James and seven-year-old Ellen are in the most terrible state. Richie is ten and Joanna is three, they've been getting worse each day. That leaves Kate, eighteen, and May, who is nine. They seem to be untouched by the symptoms.'

'I will arrange for the sick children to go to hospital immediately.'

Matilda was at first stunned by this news but slowly regained her composure as she rubbed the back of her hands in agitation and concern, 'People only go to hospital to die. Is that what you are saying? That there is nothing you can do for them? Just come inside and see them, doctor,' she took him by the arm and tried to drag him further into the hut.

'Maybe you can give me some medicine for them. I'll look after them, you know I will.'

'Miss Schafer, please, calm yourself. Look at this disgusting shack. Who can tell what assortment of diseases these children have picked up. In hospital they will be clean and well fed.' He put his hand on hers and said sternly, 'Can't you understand I am giving them a chance to live.'

Her hand dropped from his arm like lead. With all the anguish and despair Doctor Robinson had dealt with in his career he had never witnessed the strength of such a dynamic personality as Matilda Schafer dissolve before his eyes. Throughout the community she had regularly been a tower of strength for anyone in difficulties. But she stood before him now upset, helpless and alone.

To receive pity in this vulnerable state would be abhorrent to her, so instead of showing any he said gruffly, 'I will not walk through the filth on this floor. I have other calls to make in decent homes and I will not traipse the O'Connell muck through them. Get the children ready as best you can while I arrange transport for them to the Maryborough Hospital. Good day, Matilda.

He went to leave but stopped in mid step and turned to face her, 'You're a good woman, Matilda Schafer. Not many would bother with children like these. Believe me I will do all I can for them.' He tipped his hat to her and strode out the door.

*

Doctor Lee Garde walked briskly through the hospital grounds from his home to his office; his mind swirling to prioritise the events of the last twenty-four hours. As Superintendent of the Maryborough Hospital, he was required to oversee the urgent preparations to accept the O'Connell children, who were quite possibly contagious.

As if that wasn't enough one of the nurses had just filed a complaint of assault with the hospital board against the fire brand resident surgeon, Doctor Henry Croker Garde, who was also his half uncle, just to make things a little more complicated.

Doctor Graham Dixon had just reported the suspicious symptoms of his patient Mrs. Letitia Edwards who recently had contact with these children and whose symptoms now mirrored theirs. While Mrs. Edwards could be safely attended to by her husband and Doctor Dixon in her own home it was the opinion of Doctor Robinson that these children, in such unfortunate circumstances, would not survive if left in the filth of their cottage.

The suspicious nature of their illness meant that an isolation ward had to be prepared to protect the other patients while the severity of the children's condition required that the full complement of staff be available.

On reaching his office Doctor Lee Garde immediately prepared to write a letter to Nurse Cecelia Bauer who was on leave at home in Tiaro fourteen miles south of town to prepare for her upcoming wedding. He would explain the situation and ask her to return to work as a matter of urgency.

Nurse Adelaide Wiles had already volunteered to care for the children in the isolation ward. She was intelligent and cheery, the perfect choice for nursing a family of ill children. Cecelia Bauer was conscientious and nurturing. He knew the two nurses would work well together in a semi-isolated ward until this was over. He had just finished his letter when there was a knock at his door.

'Come in,' he responded a little preoccupied as he was checking the wording of his letter.

'Excuse me, Doctor Garde, the O'Connell children have just arrived in the hospital grounds.'

'Thank you, Nurse Sprague. Keep them away from other patients and help Nurse Wiles get them settled in the isolation ward. From my information they will need a cleanup. Bath the ones that are well enough, and bed wash the others. Then have all their clothes incinerated.' He held out the letter, 'Have this hand delivered immediately.'

PRESENT DAY 5 - MAY 28.

Before reciting the day's story for Cole Sue had arrived at the rendezvous site early for a change and parked in front of Cole's four-wheel drive. By the time she'd thumped her door open Cole was emerging from the site of the Edwards' house carrying tiny glass vials filled with dirt. As Sue stumbled out of her car Cole greeted her and opened the back door of his vehicle. Sue stood next to him and curtly asked, 'What were you doing on that property?'

'Collecting samples for evidence of plague.' Without looking at Sue Cole calmly took a plastic bag from his metal briefcase and in his meticulous handwriting made a note on the bag.

'Did you ask permission to walk all over their place?'

'Sue, please, do not exaggerate, I only walked on some of it.'

He sealed the bag and carefully placed it next to one marked "O'Connell Site". I did not disturb them. I think they have gone to work already. It would be irresponsible of me to worry local residents by telling them why I need the soil samples.'

Sue remained icy, 'Well, I think it's very rude to be walking around a home without permission.'

Cole looked surprised at her stance but smiled, closed the car door and leaned against it, 'Sue, I am sorry if you think I was taking liberties, but you must understand that I am investigating this outbreak for a reason, a very important reason, and time is running out. If sometimes I need to take a shortcut, please be confident that it is for the greater good. What benefit is there in telling people that I'm looking for evidence of the Black Death in their front yard? It would upset them for no reason.'

'Well,' Sue mulled this over for a moment. 'I suppose there was no harm done.'

'None at all. Friends?' Cole held out his hand which Sue shook, and peace was restored temporarily.

'So where shall we meet tomorrow then?'

'I'll be at your motel at 8.30am. I thought you might like to get out of the town for a while and experience some Australian bush. We can visit Blackmount near Tiaro, a little town twenty-two kilometers south of Maryborough. Nurse Cecelia Bauer was staying with her parents before her wedding when she received the letter from the hospital that sealed her death.'

'Yes, a tragic waste of a vibrant young life. I am beginning to see why you are so passionate about getting more recognition for Nurses Bauer and Wiles.'

'Really? Well stick around Cole there's a hell of a lot more to come yet.'

*

Once back in his motel room Cole called out to Chappie,

'What says, Lurman?'

Chappie walked in from the verandah while putting the final polish on his size thirteen army boots.

'Not much. Lurman has apparently exhausted the patience of the archive staff and come up with bugger all.'

'What about hospital records?'

'Don't have any, they reckon. Lost in the flood maybe, they said, or destroyed earlier, but there are no

Maryborough Hospital records for that year in the Queensland State Archives.'

'Well, that is odd, not to mention a nuisance. It might have helped us to understand this disease a little better if we actually had the notes and thoughts of the doctors as it was happening. They would have been the only modern-day accounts of a pneumonic plague epidemic. Blast their sloppy record keeping! We would not have had this problem if the outbreak had happened in a Dutch colony. Beautiful records they kept, with meticulous details.'

'Yea, well, no argument here, but the fact remains that Lurman had a damn hard job finding any reference of pneumonic plague anywhere but, little French ferret that he is, he is bringing back some gold.'

'Ah, good news at last.'

'Yep, Lurman has found some pretty hot letters of condemnation and accusations between the Maryborough Hospital and the Health Department. Some of the handwritten comments are even in the borders of those letters and are well worth a read.'

'Well, well, something with which to look forward. But why is it so difficult to find a record of pneumonic plague in the State Archives? Is it just government inefficiency or is it deliberate? I mean listen to this article, Chappie.

*"Maryborough Chronicle June 24. THE PLAGUE OUTBREAK. Who is to Blame? The O'Connell children were sent to the hospital **before** anything had occurred to **arouse suspicion**, and because it was evident to Doctor Robertson, who was called in, that they would get no proper attention in their own neglected and motherless home."*

Cole handed the paper to Chappie, 'Arouse suspicion? We

have never researched such a secretive plague epidemic.'
Chappie read the article again, 'Yea, so true. By the way the sewer dig is finished and all back to normal. Our German ice queens are enjoying their stay in an air-conditioned room outside of town until we're ready for them.'

DAY SIX - Cecelia

MAY 29, 1905.

"All day long carts rumbled through the city streets

while their drivers shouted, "Bring out your dead!"

Anon.

Matilda Schafer was taking advantage of the sunny morning to hang out the newly washed clothes. From the corner of her eye, she caught the slightest of movements. Richard O'Connell was standing near the side fence nervously playing with his cloth cap. He hesitantly advanced a few steps but kept a respectful distance, 'I owe ya an apology, Tilly. I should never've spoken to ya tha way I did when ya came visiting tha children. Now ya know why I was so upset with John still laying there and no money ta bury him.'

Matilda put down her washing and took the pegs out of her mouth, 'You should have told me, Richard. Something could have been arranged.'

'Does no good arguing tha toss now. I've come about Kate and May. They're with you still?'

'Yes.'

'I's been told they're sick.'

'Not like your other children dear, they only have a cold.'

'No matter, Tilly, I want them sent ta hospital just in case. Tha' gossip on tha' wharves is they've got plague, and George says that Lettie is sick after lookin' after John. People don't think so Tilly, but I do love them kids. But since their Mam died, I just need a quick drink on my way home from work, just ta help me forget a bit, and then, well you've seen how it is.'

Matilda nodded. She knew how it was. When her brother Bill had been on his way home from the wharves, he'd come across Richard in such a drunken condition that he could not find his way home. Bill had guided him to his front door and left him for the children to look after.

'You'll see to it tha' they goes into hospital?'

'Of course, but don't you want to see them?'

'I wouldn't know what ta say. But tell 'em I'm doing this for their own good.'

He slapped his cloth cap on his head and retraced his steps down the side of the house and headed for the wharves.

*

At the family property in Blackmount, seventeen miles south of Maryborough, Nurse Cecelia Bauer was quickly finishing her packing. She glanced regularly down the driveway for the telltale swirl of dust that would announce the arrival of her fiancé's buggy.

Annie Bauer, Cecelia's devoted mother, hovered in the background attempting to help but not really wanting her daughter to leave. She too was keeping an eye on the driveway.

With a slight note of urgency Annie broached the subject for the last time, 'Must you really go, Cecelia? You are on holiday. Surely, it's not that much of an emergency that they have to drag you away from your wedding arrangements.'

'Mother, we went through this when the letter arrived from Doctor Lee Garde. He would not have asked me to come back to work if it was not urgent.' Cecelia moved to Annie's side and linked arms. 'Mother, it is a family of young children. They need to be nursed around the clock.'

'Well, what's wrong with them, something contagious obviously if it's a whole family?'

'They've been admitted as Dengue Fever cases. With care and attention, we will all be back in our homes soon. Please don't worry.'

A tear betrayed Annie's brave composure. She trembled as she hugged her daughter tightly, 'I know it is your calling dear, but your father and I love you so very much. I can't bear the thought of you catching one of those terrible diseases.'

From outside Felix shouted, 'Buggy's here.'

Cecelia kissed her mother on the cheek, 'I'll be back soon. Please don't worry.'

They collected the luggage and headed outside just in time to catch the tail end of a conversation between Cecelia's father Felix and her fiancé, William Hastings.

'How's your new bay mare going, Will?'

Will was affectionately stroking the mare's nose, 'Just fine, Felix. Still a little jittery in town but she'll calm down with practice.'

Felix loaded the luggage expertly on the back of the buggy,

'Ah well, dropping Celi off at the hospital today will do your mare good then.'

After hugs and a kisses all round Felix helped his daughter climb into the buggy, 'Be careful, Celi love. We'll see you in a few weeks.'

Will jumped in next to her. At the flick of the reins, they trotted down the driveway waving goodbye.

Cecelia's mother waited on the doorstep until her daughter was out of sight.

'Come on Annie. No good standing here all day.'

'Felix, this is so irregular. I'm sure there is more to it than Cecelia knows. But she will not entertain the idea.'

'Annie, they are a hospital. They'll take all the precautions necessary.'

'I can only hope that you are right, Felix.'

*

Will looked over at Cecelia and gave her an exaggerated once over, 'I do like that green spotted dress; it always looks so cool and clean even on a dusty road. Isn't it the one your mother made for your birthday?'

'You know very well that it is. Thank you for the compliment but I know you are making small talk because you want to discuss something serious and you're hedging. Out with it.'

'Alright, Celi, what do you think all this is about?'

'Being called back to the hospital, you mean?'

'Yes. It's odd, isn't it?'

'Will, there is a Dengue Fever epidemic at the moment.'

'I know it's in the papers nearly every day.'

'Well, it's just unfortunate that a whole family of children has caught it at the same time. Will, you know a hospital is a sterile and regimented place. Those poor little things will be scared enough without a dozen different people poking and prodding them every day. It will be much easier on the children just to have one nurse staying with them all the time.'

'You may have a point, Celi.'

'And the silver lining is, if the children feel comfortable, they will get better faster, and I will be home sooner.'

'I'm just glad you are not a lawyer, Celi. No one would have a chance against your smooth-talking skills.'
He flashed her a teasing grin that, for a heartbeat, revealed the freckled faced boy just under the surface of the manly face. She squeezed his hand.

The dirt track wove its way through acres of lush green cane fields topped by feathery purple flumes. In a clearing close to the train line thin wisps of blue smoke escaped from the blackened roofs of some Kanaka huts.

Cecelia suddenly became serious, 'Will, the Kanaka compound is not empty. I thought when the Pacific Islands Labourers Act was brought in that it was compulsory to send all the Kanakas back to the island from where they had come?'

'You are right, Celi, but they can apply to remain here if they want. Most of them have been put on the transport ships going out of Maryborough but, for whatever reason, these ones want to stay here and work the sugar cane for wages.'

'That is good, isn't it?' Cecelia asked, 'They are sturdy workers, and they know the job.'
Will's tanned face lit up with a cheeky smile, 'Oh, so now you're a Sugar Cane manager! Yes, they'll do ok. Now enough about work, let's talk wedding plans. That should keep us going until we get into town.'

PRESENT DAY 6 - MAY 29.

'Sorry Sue, you are doing a fantastic job. Out here in the bush you make these people come alive for me. But I really do need to interrupt. This Kanaka business, it could be very relevant to my research. I really do not know much about the Kanaka trade in Australia. Can you give me more details?'

'Sure, but you told me your time was limited. I didn't want to waste it with unnecessary details.'

'That I realize, but it could offer another explanation as to how the pneumonic plague seemed to suddenly appear in Maryborough.'

Sue looked doubtful but Cole had settled himself with arms folded and was waiting.

'OK, if you say so. In a nutshell a trader named Captain Robert Towns began importing islanders from Solomon Islands, New Hebrides, Torres Strait Islands and Papua New Guinea in 1873. At the time it was believed that white men would die if they worked in such hot conditions. Captain Town's answer was to recruit islanders to work in the Queensland sugar cane and cotton fields. Sometimes they came willingly but many were kidnapped and locked in the putrid hold of the ship for the entire voyage.'

'Now that was the practice of 'blackbirding', I am correct? From what I have read it was responsible for the brutal deaths of many islanders.'

'That's right, for the next forty years, over 800 ships visited the South Seas Islands and issued about 62,000 work contracts to people labeled Kanakas.'

'Sue, did you know that Kanaka is the Hawaiian word for boy? That being so did they take women as well?'

'Yes, men and women from all over the South Seas were forced to work as slaves in the fields of Queensland cane and cotton plantations.'

'So why were they sent back?'

'If you get the folder I gave you with all the historic info in it there's a page on the Kanaka trade.'
Cole reached into the back seat and withdrew the folder.

'If you read these notes now it will make it clearer for you.'
Cole took the notes and started to read out aloud,

"PACIFIC ISLANDS LABOURERS ACT - The decision to stop the labour trade in the 1890's created a furore of public debate. The sugar lobby desperately wanted to keep its source of cheap labour, while labour unions saw them as a threat to their members. Under pressure the government put its 'White Australia Policy' into effect in 1904, began repatriation of south sea islanders still in the country (with some exceptions) and forbade the recruitment of any others."

"IMMIGRATION RESTRICTION ACT LEGISTATION – 1901 (CWTH) Receives royal assent on 23/12/01. It was described as an act "to place certain restrictions on immigration and to provide for the removal from the commonwealth of prohibited immigrants."

"PACIFIC ISLANDS LABOURERS ACT - 1901-1906 (CWTH) Decreed that there should be no further entry of islanders after 31/4/901. After that date deportation was to follow, with some exemptions."

'Thanks Sue, you have certainly done some in-depth

research. This just might bring to light another possible theory as to the cause of the pneumonic plague outbreak. Shall we head back to town now and we can discuss this new theory on the way?'

For the first few kilometers of cane fields and beef cattle Cole concentrated on the road and said nothing. Sue was by now familiar with his periods of silence and took the opportunity to study the beauty of the Australian bush and rural properties.

Eventually Cole stirred and opened the discussion with, 'A large number of the seaports on the south seas islands were in the grip of bubonic plague at the time you say the Kanaka's were being returned.'

'So?'

'Well with pneumonic plague the time from infection to death is four to six days. Far too long for the disease to have been carried by an infected human from Hong Kong, which was also suffering a plague epidemic at the time, as it took weeks to sail to Australia. On the other hand, some of the close islands were only days from Maryborough.'

'Cole, do you really have a theory or are you . . .'

'Just talking for the sake of it? No, no, I have a valid theory based on the incubation time. Captains getting paid to take Kanakas back to their islands would not return to Maryborough empty if there were passengers or cargo to bring back for a tidy profit.'

'Yes, so where does the plague come in.'

'A passenger might have come on board already infected. If they developed a cough and fever during the short voyage, it would not create much concern. If they kept to themselves, which is very possible as the crews on these ships were not always the most savory specimens, then it would not have had a chance to spread. John worked as a clerk on the wharves. He may have had close enough contact with that person when they docked to have breathed in the "Yersinia Pestis" bacterium.'

'So where did this mystery person go without causing an epidemic?

'A few possibilities there; they might have caught a stagecoach and headed out to an isolated rural property and died there. By the time they were found nobody would know what killed them. Or if they were Chinese or Kanaka, and before you interrupt me . . .' Cole held up his hand in front of Sue's open mouth, 'Remember, some Kanakas preferred to stay on in the fields, but some worked on the ships as crew. They helped with the repatriation of their fellow islanders. If a sick Kanaka or Chinaman headed home through the cane fields and died en route by the time they were found, if ever, the cause of death would not be known, and the threat of spreading died with the victim. As you are aware the death of a Chinaman or a Kanaka at the time was not something that required a report to the authorities. I am not saying this is what happened, but I must consider any possibility.'

'Are you aware that the Kanakas were not only treated at the Maryborough Hospital but had their own ward?'

'No, I did not. That was very compassionate for the times.'

'In fact, on May 11, just two weeks before John O'Connell's death, there was a Kanaka admitted to the hospital. His employer, a Mr. Timbrell, refused to cover any costs involved. But the Polynesian Inspector stated that the employer was responsible for all costs.'

'Do we know for what ailment the Kanaka was being

treated, perhaps in hospital records or the annual report?'

'If they still exist for 1905, I can't find them. Every time I visit the Brisbane State Archives with another angle to find some records from the time, I get told that they've probably been destroyed during the big flood in 1974 or earlier. The State Archive building was in the city then and when the Brisbane River broke its banks, it, like many other buildings housing public records, had their basements and many of their floors go underwater. And before you ask, no it was not a regular thing. It was a chain of events that caused it. It has happcned again, but of course the damage is done or at least that's what gets the blame when they can't find something.'

'Or when they prefer not to allow something to be public,' added Cole.

'Well, I suppose that does happen in some countries but not here, Aussie's are not into all the conspiracy and cover up stuff. Anyway, why bother, it was over one hundred years ago?'

Cole smiled slightly and gave her a look that made her feel like a naive child, 'We are nearly back at my motel; tomorrow is day seven of this plague event, where shall we meet?'

'I'll meet you in front of the main entrance of the old hospital building. I pointed it out to you before.'

'Yes, I know the one. Thank you for the graphic descriptions. You have a knack for bringing a story alive. Ah, here is your car. See you tomorrow.'

As Sue struggled with her car door she noticed two men, in what looked army fatigues, jump out of a dark green land rover as Cole parked his red four-wheel-drive in front of his motel room. They did not salute but their posture and bearing gave the impression of soldiers reporting something of interest to a superior.

A huge barrel-chested man with a crop of flaming red hair came out of Cole's room dressed in board shorts and singlet. He obviously also commanded respect from the two strangers. He handed them some papers and with a nod they drove off.

I suppose that's Chappie Sue thought. Cole said he was here with a friend. Something is going on he's not telling me about as the stuck door released its grip and violently swung open.

DAY SEVEN – The Lolly Jar

MAY 30, 1905.

'Bodies were heaped by the hundreds

like goods in a ship's hold.'

Giovanni Boccaccio, *Decameron (1353)*

'Hello, Ellen. Do you remember me, Nurse Celi? I was here last night before you went to sleep.'

'Yes, I remember your voice when the coughing kept waking me up.'

'That's right. Now I will be with you all day and night to help you get better. That is my camp bed, close to you, so I can hear you call me anytime.'

'I sat with John all day and night too. I tried to make him better, but his cough just kept getting worse and worse until he died.'

She turned her head to look at the red bottlebrush growing outside the window, 'We are going to die just like John, Nurse Celi. But I am glad you are here.'

'John was not in hospital, my angel, with the doctors and nurses to make him better.'

'Will the doctors make us better, Nurse Celi?'

'We are doing everything we can to make sure you all get better. And your job is to try and eat a little bit then rest. Will you do that for me?'

Ellen nodded as Cecelia held her hand and stroked her brow. Slowly the child succumbed to the effects of fever and the exhaustion of constant, body racking coughing. Each rattling breath echoed through the isolation ward. It did not take special training to know that the little girl's death was imminent. Cecelia gently eased her hand from Ellen's grasp and turned to talk to James when Ellen asked drowsily, 'I know James is sick like me but how are Joanna and Richie?'

'They are enjoying the food, and the picture books Nurse Rose bought in.'

'Richie was always hungry. We could never fill him up. Joanna is just a baby. She has never seen a picture book.' Ellen gave a faint smile and drifted into a fitful sleep.

'Nurse Cecelia?' Cecelia turned in her chair to face her other patient.

'Yes, James.'

'I heard Nurse Sprage talking in the other ward. She was asking the doctor where she should put May and Kate. Are they sick too?'

'Doctor believes that they only have a cold, and they will be better soon. They are in hospital just in case.'

'Can they visit us, especially Joanna, she really misses Kate? Just for a minute?'

'No, dear. You are brave enough to understand that none of us can leave this ward, including myself and Nurse Rose, until you all get better. Even your food is left outside the ward door for us to collect.'

James was sweating profusely. His once handsome face was a pasty white backdrop to two black circles around his sunken, glazed eyes. He was rolling his head in anger and frustration, becoming irrationally upset over the issue, a sure sign that the fever was moving into the delirium stage. Cecelia gently held his head still,

'That's it, James. That's it. Shh, shh. Listen to my voice.

'When John became sick you took over as head of the

family. You looked after the young ones. Although Kate is the eldest she was away working nearly every day. And I heard that you cared so much you defied your father's order not to leave the house when John's body was lying on the floor because you needed to find more food for Joanna, Richie, Ellen and May. They are too young to be roaming the streets alone.'

James' voice was faint but coherent, 'You heard Ellen just now; Richie was always hungry, and Joanna just loves a lolly. Sometimes, if Mrs. Lanne from the corner store was in a good mood, I could sweet-talk her into giving me one of those coloured boiled lollies. I'd smile at her and say, "but it's for my baby sister, Joanna, Mrs. Lanne. Of all the lollies in Maryborough she loves yours the best." Most times she'd chase me out of the shop with a broom but if I picked just the right day, she'd reach into a huge glass jar a pull out the biggest and the reddest one and drop it into my pocket. When I got home Joanna would have to guess which pocket it was in. She loved . . .' he started coughing deeply, gut-wrenchingly, 'that game.'

James lay back on the pillow fighting for breath and clutching his chest. Another coughing fit turned the thick sputum crimson with blood. Cecelia held him firmly around the shoulders until the coughing subsided and he lay exhausted against her with his head on her shoulder. She stroked his cheek as she rocked him gently back and forth while crooning softly in his ear,

'I'm going to ask Nurse Sprage to leave a lolly each on your dinner tray tomorrow, those red ones with the white stripes. If you sit it on your tongue and don't chew, it will last for hours and hours.'

James' breathing had slowed to a more regular rhythm, but his chest rattled ominously. Cecelia laid him down on the pillow where he remained weakly plucking at his congested chest.

'For your sake and theirs, James, you must rest. Let go of the reins for a while. Nurse Rose and I will look after all of you.'

As Cecelia wrote up her day notes in readiness to hand over to Nurse Rose Wiles for the night shift, she prayed that Doctor Lee Garde would find a cure soon. If not, Ellen and James had very little time to live.

PRESENT DAY 7 - MAY 30.

As Sue recounted the events leading up to the deaths of the O'Connell children, she and Cole had walked from the site of the recently demolished old red brick morgue to the front of a stately two-story building. A Poinciana tree with wildly spreading branches offered a shady spot to sit directly in front of the building's entrance. Scattered on the trim lawn the last of its crimson blossoms lay. An atmosphere of sunny tranquility belied the building's horrific past.

'Directly in front of us, Cole, on the ground floor is the isolation ward were the O'Connell children, Nurse Bauer and Nurse Wiles died so agonizingly.'

'My God, it is such a lovely old building; elegant staircase, broad shady veranda's, it looks more like a resort than a hospital.'

'Nurse Cecelia Bauer had died by the time the train pulled into Maryborough with the Colmslie plague nurses on board from Brisbane. This left only Nurse Rose Adelaide Wiles to be cared for which they did, doused up with a shot of Yersinia's Serum, wearing waterproof overalls, goggles, respirators, and rubber gloves. Where's your folder?'

Cole handed it to her, and Sue flicked quickly through the pages of newspaper articles until, 'Ah, here it is.'

"The nurses from Colmslie were in complete isolation, sleeping on the verandah, exposed to wind and weather, interrupted in their sleep by the health men, doing their rounds with the disinfectants and fumigators. Telegrams were always coming from their friends urging them to resign, but no, they stuck to their guns like Britons, and their

work was beyond praise." What burns me up is that when they arrived back in Brisbane they were greeted as heroines, but the bodies of our dedicated nurses were dumped in lime, buried in three-meter graves and forgotten.'

'Do you have a theory as to why this has happened?'

'Of course! It was politics. I think the authorities needed to keep it quiet. At the time the state of New South Wales was refusing to accept any products from Queensland because of the plague outbreaks and they were pretty much our only market at the time. Queensland farmers and their families were suffering severely. To make matters worse discussions to lift the ban were in progress at the very time this outbreak occurred, placing everyone from the Premier down to the Maryborough doctors in a difficult position. Doctor Baxter-Tyrie seems to be the man they sent in to keep a tight lid on things.'

Cole nodded as he considered her words seriously, 'That is a valid conclusion but why the lack of recognition these days? So far all I have seen to honor the Maryborough nurses is that building around the corner with Maryborough Bauer-Wiles Community Health Centre on the sign and yet an impressive and rather expensive statue of Mary Poppins has been recently erected in the main street. Why? Because the author was born here?'

'Exactly Cole, Maryborough relies heavily on the tourist dollar. Association with an international character like Mary Poppins is good for business.'

'But her family moved away when she was only two.
Sue gave him a very surprised and quizzical look.
Cole answered her look with apparent guileless honesty,
'What? I studied up on some Maryborough history during

my flight here.'

'If you say so.' Sue shrugged her shoulders. 'Anyway, council and businesses feel that it is better than being known as the only site in Australia to have suffered an outbreak of the deadliest plague in history. None of the official powers-that-be wants to be reminded of that, or that the city fathers at the time may have been forced to keep it quiet because of the embargo. Sue put her hand up indicating words for billboard sign, "Welcome to Maryborough, bring out your dead!" is not considered a good marketing slogan. I have letters from 1905 between the Home Secretary 's Office, the Commissioner of Public Health and the local doctors, slinging mud at each other like you wouldn't believe, blaming each other for the death of the nurses.'

'I think I am with you now, Sue. To honour the Nurses Bauer and Wiles, as they deserve, would mean opening this outbreak to national and international scrutiny. A clever journalist just might draw parallels between any government cover up in those days to the Health Department's handling of some very contentious medical issues recently on the front-page news.'

As he spoke Cole turned to face Sue. Her face said it all. Something he'd said or the way he said it had fanned the flames of suspicion again, 'What's your real interest in this disease, Cole. You say you're a medical researcher, but you poke around people's property like a private investigator, and you talk like a politician.'

Cole remained silent for a moment. He studied the building before him, then looked down at his hands before replying,

'Sue, what do you actually know about pneumonic

plague?'

'Well, when I first started this campaign, I asked a few doctors about it and I was told it was a dead disease, that antibiotics now had it under control. I tried to get information from people at various levels of the health department, but they were no help either.'

'I see. Many people, even many Western doctors, are under the assumption that plague is no longer a threat. For bubonic plague, yes, there is often a good survival rate.'

'Survival rate? What are you saying? That we still have outbreaks, even today?'

'Most definitely, cases of pneumonic plague are reported regularly from Africa, Asia, South America, Madagascar, United States, China, Mongolia, and Viet Nam. Parts of China even have signs around picnic areas warning people not to leave rubbish behind because it encourages rats, and they carry the plague. In the tropical and subtropical areas of the world, in particular, northern and southern Africa, some parts of North America it has invaded the populations of rodents, squirrels, and lagomorphs.'

'What the hell are they?'

'Oh, sorry Sue, that means rabbits and hares.'

'God Cole, I had no idea. But these have been isolated cases, right?'

'Not necessarily. In September 1994 the town of Surat in India reported an epidemic of pneumonic plague. Several countries closed their borders to Indian travelers and cargo was turned back. All flights to and from India were cancelled. The Centers for Disease Control and Prevention upgraded surveillance in the United States for imported pneumonic plague. Plague information was compiled and quickly distributed across the United States to public health officials by electronic mail. Quarantine surveillance was upgraded. With the assistance of the air crews and security, people were detained who exhibited pneumonic plague symptoms during their flights. This coordinated response to an international health emergency has actually served as a model for handling future disease threats.'

'There you go talking like a politician. So where do you fit into all this?

'Do you mind if we walk and talk to the car? I have an appointment to keep.'
Cole took back his folder and continued his explanation as they walked towards the street, 'Plague is currently a notifiable disease under the International Health Regulations. Cases reported to the World Health Organization between 1989 and 2003 alone totaled 38,310 across twenty-five countries. Luckily these were in isolated, containable areas. There is no vaccine or inoculation to prevent catching pneumonic plague and the one for bubonic is dicey at best.'

'But Cole the antibiotics these days, don't they work?'

'For bubonic plague there is a reasonable survival, and it is easily recognisable even by laymen. But pneumonic plague must be treated within the first twenty-four hours or death will follow usually in four to six days. Pneumonic is rarely diagnosed in time because it looks like flu, and it seems to flare up from nowhere. That is where I come in.'

'Doing what exactly?'

'Plague and the causes for outbreaks are not understood especially in its pneumonic form. For example, India had not reported a case of pneumonic plague for twenty-eight years and then an epidemic broke out. Why? This is part of my job. To study all the known confirmed outbreak sites and compile the necessary information. I need things like soil samples, temperature, rainfall details, local health department protocols when dealing with contagious diseases, rat populations and local medical treatments. All this information will be compared with other outbreaks to try and decipher what conditions or elements cause the disease to flare up again and again.'

As soon as they reached Cole's car, he opened the door and wound down the window to let out the hot air. They were standing next to his open driver's side door when Sue asked, 'Cole the India outbreak you said was in 1994 does that mean no other major epidemics have happened since then.'

'Not at all. Apart from the deliberate use of pneumonic plague as a bio-weapon outbreaks have been reported in Madagascar where hundreds of deaths have occurred since 2011 and it is not yet under control, United States reports deaths each year. Since 2005 international authorities have been battling repeated pneumonic plague outbreaks in the Democratic Republic of the Congo involving workers in a diamond mine in Zobia. It is a politically volatile area, and communications often cease for long periods, but pneumonic plague deaths are constantly being recorded in the Bas-Uele and Ituri areas.

'Ituri? You were there not long ago. You told me a story about the two mothers. Their sons were in trouble with the chief just like my son was in trouble with the headmaster.' Cole effortlessly swung up into the driver's seat while talking, 'Once the Congo authorities had the infected areas sealed off and the isolation centers set up, I was reassigned to Maryborough.'

He closed the door and leaned his arm out of the window.

'I really have to go now, but if you are interested, we can discuss this further tomorrow.' He gave her an engaging smile. 'Sue, I want you to know that your local knowledge has been invaluable. I hope you understand now why I am a bit nosey, as you put it. Where shall we meet up tomorrow?'

'Well, my boys have got something on at school they want me to watch. I'll have to leave a bit early if you don't mind. Oh, and the day after in Maryborough is Heritage Market Day, so all the heritage places are open that might be of interest to you, it's close to the old wharf area as well.'

'That could be informative. Chappie and I have some research to do anyway, so it will work in well. In the morning, we meet in front of the old plague ward, yes?'

Sue nodded. Cole waved and drove off leaving Sue to digest the overload of plague information he had imparted.

DAY EIGHT – Soul's of the Dead

MAY 31, 1905.

"And the (death) bells seemed hoarse with the continual

tolling, until at last they quite cease."

Daniel Defoe, *A Journal of the Plague Year (1722)*

Nurse Cecelia Bauer's day notes: 'On this day May 31, 1905, Ellen Bridget O'Connell seven years eight months and James O'Connell fifteen years five months died. Their illness lasted approximately four days and began with symptoms of headache and vomiting, followed by fever, delirium, and pericardial pain. Sputum became loose and watery followed soon afterwards by death.'

Her tears ran unchecked and dripped from her chin onto the page, causing the ink to run. Cecelia dabbed at it with blotting paper. Nurse Rose Wiles stood in the doorway for a moment watching the torment on her colleague's face. She did not move to give physical comfort but instead offered words of advice gleaned from some difficult experiences as a young nurse herself.

'Cecelia, please do not accuse me of being callous but an essential element of good nursing is the ability to accept the death of innocents.'

She sat down in front of Cecelia and took her by the hands,

'Dear, you have done everything humanly possible to help them, now you must look to the living. Would you like me to prepare the bodies?'

'No!' Snapped Cecelia as she pulled her hands away.

Rose was taken aback at this uncharacteristic outburst.

'Oh, Rose, I'm so sorry. I mean, I do appreciate your

offer, but I would like to prepare them myself.'

'As you wish dear, but keep this in mind, if you are going to get so upset over every patient who dies then it is my belief you have chosen the wrong profession. Do what you must without tears, for the sake of the other children.'

'Yes, Rose. I will.' Cecelia wiped away the tear tracks and started the last duty she could perform for Ellen and James.

'Good, I will call for a wardsman to leave a trolley outside. We should be able to dispatch the corpses to the morgue before Richie and Joanna wake up.'

Rose knew from the look on Cecelia's face that she was going to object to the use of the word 'corpses' so she added quickly in a flat businesslike tone,

'Cecelia, we do this job to help the living, the souls of the dead are resting in God's hands. Their mortal remains are 'corpses' to the doctors. They are to be studied, autopsied, or dissected, whatever the doctors consider necessary. That is the reality of the situation.'

'Yes, Rose. Yes, I, ah, I do know that. Thank you for understanding. I will be all right now.'

*

In his capacity as the Medical Superintendent of the Maryborough Hospital, Doctor Lee Garde called an urgent meeting to discuss the sudden increase in deaths from this mystery disease. Attending the meeting was Doctor Cairns Penny, the Government Medical Officer of Health for Maryborough. Doctor Penny was very active in local Navel matters. His distinctive military bearing was commonly seen silhouetted against the setting sun as he stood proudly on the bow of a Navel whale boat supervising maneuvers practice on the Mary River. Also in attendance at this important meeting was Doctor Graham Dixon, a pedantic and highly respected private practitioner. Doctor Dixon, for the last few days, had been attending Mrs. Letitia Edwards, the kindly woman present at the death of her young neighbour, John O'Connell. Mrs. Edwards died a few hours before, taking the death rate for the day to three and four in total so far, from a contiguous and as yet unidentified disease.

As Doctor Dixon and Doctor Penny lived three doors apart on Sussex Street, they were not only colleagues they had become friends. Over the last few days, in particular, they had frequented each other's homes to muse, strictly between themselves, over the death of John O'Connell and the illness of Mrs. Edwards.

In a rare deviation from the norm, Doctor Lee Garde had requested all staff to clear the office until called to return. On hearing the approaching voices, he opened the door himself and waited as the two men traversed the length of the hallway. They looked as opposite as two men could be. Doctor Graham Dixon was short and stocky. His balding greying hair was over-compensated for by a luxurious black moustache. He took short, measured steps and was wearing his usual attire of black suit and tie. From a distance he had the appearance of a fusty old dullard but to meet him face to face one could see in his bright, intelligent eyes compassion and dependability.

Doctor Cairns Penny was tall and slim with a thick head of silvery hair that he kept cropped short under his naval cap. He wore his snowy white uniform with pride and strode down the hallway in long determined strides. He kept his emotions, but not his opinions, under the strictest of control. Without the usual preliminaries Doctor Lee Garde ushered them into his office.

'Take a seat gentleman, I assume you understand the seriousness of our problem?'

Always prepared to take the lead in any situation Doctor Cairns Penny opened the discussion in his commandingly deep and well-modulated voice, 'I understand that two more of the O'Connell children died in hospital today.'

'Correct,' stated Doctor Lee Garde. 'I signed their death certificates as Bronchopneumonia but that was before we knew of the death of Mrs. Letitia Edwards. The obvious contagious quality of this disease demands from us more stringent controls. I issued instructions that the remaining O'Connell children be isolated and placed in the sole charge of Nurse Cecelia Bauer. Nurse Rose Wiles was overseeing that ward at night. She will share the nursing duties with Nurse Bauer, and both have been warned to take all the standard precautions.

'Thank you, Doctor Garde. Now to Doctor Dixon, your patient, Mrs. Edwards, also expired today in her own bed. Is that correct?'

In contrast to his colleague, Doctor Dixon liked to consider every word carefully before its utterance. This carefulness of speech coupled with his crisp and precise manner gave everyone he met the fullest confidence in his ability as a doctor and his integrity as a man, 'That is so. It stressed her awfully when I mentioned going to hospital. I deemed it then better if she remained comfortable in her own bed.

But, oh, how quickly she deteriorated.'

Doctor Penny placed a companionable hand on his colleague's shoulder, 'Graham, please contain your anxiety, none of us knew even this morning that we were against such a swift and deadly disease as this.'

Doctor Lee Garde nodded his agreement and added, 'We now have four deaths from what appears to be the same illness, and I have been informed that the resolute Doctor Dixon has refused to write a death certificate for the unfortunate Mrs. Edwards.'

'That is correct,' confirmed Doctor Dixon, 'I wish to formally request an autopsy on Mrs. Edwards. It is my professional opinion that we could be dealing with a very swift and virulent strain of plague.'

'In that case Doctor Dixon, you and I have a duty to report these suspicions to Mayor Dawson. Doctor Penny, I entrust this action to you.'

'I will in all haste and send a telegram directly to Doctor Burnett Ham. As the Commissioner of Public Health in Brisbane he can grant permission for an immediate post-mortem examination on the body of Mrs. Edwards.'

'Good. Doctor Dixon, you would be satisfied with this action?' asked Doctor Lee Garde.

'Certainly,' replied Doctor Dixon. 'Doctor Penny, can we anticipate an answer to your request today?'

'With my recommendation I would expect a reply granting permission by this afternoon,' announced Doctor Penny shifting in his seat. He much preferred action to conversation. Doctor Lee Garde was satisfied with what had been done so far and prepared to finish the meeting with a plan of action. 'On that assumption then, Doctor

Penny, I will immediately write a letter to the mayor stating our plague suspicions and will cause to have it delivered by hand this afternoon. I suggest also that Doctor Dixon and myself visit upon Mayor Dawson at nine am of the morrow. Then at eleven am the two of you will meet at the Edwards home and make arrangements for the postmortem examination.'

PRESENT DAY 8 - MAY 31.

Sue had finished her narration for Cole and left early to collect her boys from a sporting carnival. Moments after she had left the hospital grounds a green four-wheel-drive swung into the circular driveway towing a long white caravan. It parked under the shade of the Poinciana tree.

On the road a convoy of khaki green trucks pulled up a uniform distance apart to allow teams of men in grey overalls to jump smartly to the ground and swiftly form a straight line along the footpath. When relieved of their cargo the trucks drove off to be replaced by a semi pulling an eighteen-wheel low loader trailer.

Immediately the waiting men moved forward to start the unloading process, beginning with four large electric winches. These were carried by the first wave of men and placed at the four corners of the old plague hospital.

Cole parked his red four-wheel drive on the street where he and Chappie could survey the building, 'Shouldn't be too difficult being a two-story place,' Chappie commented.

'No, but I want this operation sealed, pumped and packed by 3pm when the schools gets out. This road clogs up like a major highway then and we do not need to stir up public suspicion. Public Relations will have plenty of that to handle soon enough.'

'Sure, Cole. Will the staff be a problem?'

'No, the official letters have been received. They know to keep away. Get things started here and meet me in the caravan. I want to have another try at contacting the Congo base.'

Chappie walked up the gravel path to the front entrance of the building, which was now swarming with men in grey overalls, and bellowed, 'Lurman, you here?'

'Oui, Oui. Just plugging in the winches.'

'Ok. Is Team A ready on the second-floor verandah?'

'Oui. All is prepared. Team B positions the sheeting as we speak.'

Chappie surveyed the winches and barked, 'Where's the bio-chamber?'

Lurman pointed, 'It waits for our signal around the back. Such an odd vehicle on the street would attract much public attention.'

Chappie nodded his approval, 'Good man. Keep it covered until the last moment. Let's get started then.'

With a shout from Lurman the winches jumped to life and the heavy sheeting was slowly dragged up the side of the building until it reached the first floor.

On the verandah a line of grey overalled men pushed the sheeting away from the building to stop it catching on the overhanging verandah roof. From there on it flowed smoothly over the apex and glided unaided to the ground.

Experts moved in to seal and fold the sheeting corners to ensure that the air now trapped in the building could not escape back into its surrounds. Only the front door remained to be sealed.

'Good job, Lurman, shouted Chappie. 'Get your men inside then seal it up. I'll be in the van with Cole. Give me a yell when you're done.'

A group of men in yellow hazard suits with oxygen tanks were occupied with a large trolley holding carpentry equipment. They checked each item against a list before giving Lurman the thumbs up and pushing the trolley into the building. As the back of the last yellow suit disappeared into the building the doorway was sealed airtight. From behind the building the concealed bio-chamber was attached to a series of air ducts running into the building. Once activated its sole purpose was to extract and contain every particle of the dust, lint, and bacteria from the air within the building.

Chappie pulled open the caravan door and braced himself as a blast of cold air slammed his chest. He closed the door quickly, 'Where are you, Cole? It's like a freezer in here.'

'Up the back and sorry about the cold but the Germans prefer it this way.'

'Yea, well, whatever the ice queens want I suppose. Any news? Did you get onto our Congo team?'
Chappie walked past the two female German scientists who looked grudgingly up from their computer screens and in unison coolly offered a guttural welcome. Chappie nodded as he walked past but was concentrating on Cole's news update.

'Yes Chappie, and the looters in the Congo camp have been busy stealing the equipment but the local authorities have got them under guard now.'

'Well, they'd better. If they don't contain that pneumonic plague outbreak we could see panic erupting like that episode in India,' said Chappie sternly.

'Precisely. Their communications have been sporadic lately to say the least. If those miners had not panicked and run off into the jungle, we might have saved many more of them. Even the local military will have a damn hard job finding them in that jungle.'

'Yeah, but it may also be a blessing. By dying in the jungle, the disease shouldn't spread into the densely populated areas so quickly. Bless their souls,' added Chappie reverently.

'Zu-horen, zu-horen (listen),' the German scientists pointed to the internet news on a computer. 'A pneumonic plague outbreak in the Democratic Republic of the Congo has affected areas in Ituri and Bas-Uele district, Oriental province in the north of the country. This current outbreak has been centered on workers in a diamond mine in Zobia. Authorities have classified the area as 'Status Red' with a high risk of travelers contracting pneumonic plague.

The World Health Organisation is indicating that security concerns in the Democratic Republic of the Congo may lead to difficulties for personnel to gain access to the area. An immediate assessment is being carried out by a specialist team and more resources are being deployed to the area. This follows the initial report in which there were sixty-one reported deaths. A further one hundred and twenty-five contact cases are currently being followed up.

The Ministry of Health and the World Health Organization have a team in place in Zobia to undertake intensive surveillance, investigation and provision of technical support and advice on management strategies for pneumonic plague cases.

Vaccination has been proved to be ineffective in the prevention of pneumonic plague is it is a zoonotic disease that can be transmitted by direct contact with an infected person, by inhalation of the bacteria *Yersinia pestis* or it may be ingested in infected materials. Plague is endemic in many countries.'

'Ok, turn it off, we know the rest.' Chappie was interrupted by a loud banging on the caravan door.

'Cole are you in there? What the hell is going on now?' Sue's voice was shrill with anger.

In a few strides Chappie reached the door and opened it a little too quickly. Sue was knocked off her feet and landed heavily on her knees in the gravel.

Muttering dire German threats, the two scientists jumped up from their desks and pushed past Chappie like a pair of avenging Valkyries. They helped Sue to her feet and with one on each arm guided her to a nearby bench. Cole appeared with the first aid kit which they took before waving him away. Sue tried to stop them from going to so much trouble, but they smiled kindly and gently brushed her hand away.

Soon her wounds were clean and covered in suitably impressive bandages. One scientist made a final check of the first aid handy work while the other took a waiting glass of cold water from Chappie with a sharp *unbeholfen* (clumsy) and handed it to Sue. Once satisfied that they could do no more they each patted Sue softly on the shoulder and turned to face Chappie and Cole. Both men were roundly chastised in German as the first aid kit was thrust back into at Cole's hands.

'Thank you, ladies. Chappie apologizes most sincerely for his brutishness. Yes, he needs to be much more careful in the future.'

They gave Sue a last dazzling smile and retreated back into the caravan's frosty interior.

Even Cole was impressed, 'Chappie, I have never seen those two interested in anything or anyone not on the computer screen. They actually seem to have hearts.'

'And we've worked with them for years. Just might be wife material after all. We've a lot of single men on this team.'

'Sometimes, Chappie, I think you are an incorrigible romantic.'

Sue started to get up from the bench.

'Sue please stay seated, and I will answer your questions. Let me get Chappie to fetch your car.'

Sue sat down again weakly and handed Cole her car keys. As Chappie walked off to fetch it Cole positioned himself next to her.

'I was just going to pick up some pizzas for the boys when I saw all this.' Sue waved her arm in the general direction of the old hospital.

Cole looked her squarely the eyes, 'Sue it is not as mysterious as it looks. We are just taking precautions.'

'Against what?' Sue snapped.

'We need to collect samples of dirt and dust that accumulate between the walls and floorboards of these old buildings.'

'You're ripping out the walls and floor?' If Sue was angry before she was in a fury now.

'Not ripping out, it is being done very carefully and by experts.   When they are finished you would not know anything has been touched.'

'But why on earth would you need to do that?'

'To see if there is any evidence of pneumonic plague bacteria. We really do not know that much about this disease and this case offers us the most uncontaminated site we have had so far to run these types of tests. It is highly unlikely that we will find any active bacteria but just in case every bit of air and dust will go straight into the bio-tank to be analysed in a safe environment. Sue, the information I am gathering here is of international importance and just might save many lives. Please trust me on that.'

Sue had no intension of trusting Cole, or any other stranger involved in this project. Irritably she demanded, 'You've got permission to do this?'

'From the highest authorities,' Cole answered directly.

Sue ran her eyes up and down the main road, 'I'm not sure what that means but as the cops haven't been called I have to assume it's all legal.'

'Everything done here is with the utmost regard to legalities. Please understand Sue that this is necessary. You will continue to help me, yes?'

Sue avoided Cole's gaze and instead studied the closed caravan door as if somehow it held answers to her questions,

'If you are seriously interested in the lives of the pneumonic plague victims in Maryborough then you can come into town with me tomorrow. It is Heritage Market Day and all the historic buildings will be open to the public. Most of them are near the old wharf area where the plague is rumored to have been unloaded. It is also where the O'Connell father worked as a wharfie and the first victim, John O'Connell worked as a clerk. I'll go over the events that surrounded the funeral of Mrs. Edwards on the same day.'

Cole gave her hand a warm squeeze, 'That would be of invaluable assistance. I shall collect you in the morning, if that is alright, and you can guide me straight to the wharf site. Ah, here is Chappie now with your car and please accept our deepest apologies for your accident.'

As Sue's car rattled out of the hospital grounds Chappie commented, 'Cole, you know she is gonna explode when we hit the cemetery.'

'That, my friend, is a massive understatement.'

DAY NINE – An Irregular Burial

JUNE 1, 1905.

'All the power of medicines were futile against plague.'

Giovanni Boccaccio, *Decameron (1353)*

A clerk tapped briskly on the heavy timber door, 'Excuse me, Mayor Dawson Doctors Garde and Dixon are here to see you.'

'What! At nine in the morning? Which Doctor Garde is it?

'Doctor Lee Garde, Sir.'

'Ah, a bit more palatable I suppose at this hour. Wait a few moments then usher them in.'

He went to the mirror and buttoned his black coat back up across his barrel chest. As he stroked down his thinning brown hair the office doors opened. He turned smiling and greeted his visitors with an extended hand, 'Doctor Garde, Doctor Dixon, you must have something important to discuss. Sit, sit.' He swept his arm in the direction of two chairs facing his desk.

'Good morning, Mayor Dawson.' Doctor Lee Garde spoke as he took off his customary white Panama hat and settled himself into a winged armchair. 'We are here on a matter of great urgency, mayor. During the last four days we have had four deaths from a disease we now believe is a form of plague. John O'Connell of Sussex Street was the first. Two of his siblings were later admitted to the Maryborough General Hospital and both died yesterday. Doctor Dixon will now give you his report.'

Doctor Graham Dixon had perched himself on a wooden chair and lent forward as he spoke, 'Thank you, Doctor

Garde. My patient, Mrs. Letitia Edwards, also from Sussex Street, expired in her home yesterday. This Samaritan woman was with the O'Connell boy at his death. Within twenty-four hours she was ill with headache, fever, vomiting, a distressing cough and severe pain in the upper abdomen and back. By the third day she was coughing up copious amounts of watery sputum. On the fourth day she died. These people had identical symptoms; they had close contact with each other, and all died within four days. We know this disease is highly contagious and so far, has been one hundred percent fatal.'

Doctor Garde took over the conversation, 'Thank you, Doctor Dixon. Mayor Dawson, in days we could have a plague epidemic sweep though this town.'

Mayor Dawson leaned back in his chair, Doctor Garde please, there is no need to be so biblical. Dead and dying rats have preceded a plague episode for eons. Doctor Cairns Penny engaged a man solely to lay poisons in rat infested areas and I personally ordered an inspector to visit food stores, fruit shops and butchers for any new infestations. No rats caught or killed have shown any signs of illness. At Council meetings Alderman McGhie always demands a detailed account of our Rat Eradication Program. It is all on public record gentlemen.' He stood up and walked around his desk indicating that the meeting was over, 'This disease may be highly contagious and fatal and I know you will remain vigilant, but you must be circumspect in your use of the word plague.'

Doctor Lee Garde put his white Panama hat on at its customary jaunty angle and finished the interview by commenting, 'Doctor Penny has been granted permission by the health commissioner to perform a post-mortem examination of Mrs. Edwards. It has been scheduled for 11 o'clock this morning. I will be back this afternoon with the report.'

Mayor Dawson's round, red face took on a congenial facade now that everyone was leaving, 'I will look forward to it. Good day, gentlemen.'

Both men walked in silence until they were out of the Council Chambers. As they approached their buggies Doctor Garde spoke first, 'Well Graham, what did you think of our reception?'

'I think the mayor is very worried about more than the possibility of a plague epidemic.'

'Yes, I agree. Well, it is up to you and Penny now. Come to my office as soon as you have finished the postmortem.' He flicked the reins of his buggy horse, and it duly trotted off towards the hospital.

*

Doctor Cairns Penny was waiting at the designated address when Doctor Graham Dixon arrived, 'How was the meeting, Graham?' Penny greeted his friend.

'It was rather perplexing actually. Mayor Dawson seemed uncharacteristically reluctant to entertain the idea of plague.'

Penny raised a quizzical eyebrow, 'Oh, and pray tell me friend just where he studied medicine?'

'Well, precisely. That is what makes his attitude all the more mystifying. Hopefully this post-mortem will answer some questions.'

They had reached the top of the stairs where Doctor Penny took off his naval cap and respectfully tucked it smartly under his arm. He raised his hand to knock when a crowd dressed in mourning gathered behind them.

A man of the cloth reverently holding a well-worn bible opened the conversation, 'I am sorry doctors, but the post-mortem examination was declined by the deceased's family. We have just returned from performing her burial.'

Doctor Cairns Penny was incredulous, 'Without a signed death certificate? Really Reverend, that is highly illegal.'

Remaining calm and unperturbed the Reverend asked, 'Surely that was a formality only? You attended Letitia's illness yourself, Doctor Dixon. The Sexton, Nicholas Hansen, allowed the funeral procession to pass once he had established that Mrs. Edwards had seen a doctor just before her death.'

Doctor Dixon started back down the stairs, 'Reverend this is a very unfortunate situation. Very unfortunate indeed but with Doctor Penny's permission I feel now is not the time to discuss the legalities. We shall leave the family in peace.'

Courteously, the two doctors walked past the mourners. When Graham Dixon came to Arthur Edwards, he stopped to offer his deepest condolences for the man's loss. Doctor Penny offered a consolatory nod and kept walking.

PRESENT DAY 9 - JUNE 1.

As Sue wrapped up her day's story, she and Cole walked along the remnants of Maryborough's once thriving wharf area. Cole stopped and turned around to query, 'Sue, excuse me for asking this but as I am a clinical, uncreative scientist I cannot help but notice the very detailed and colourful way you present these reconstructions. It would be impossible to know so precisely what happened over a centenary ago.'

Sue's eyes flashed although her voice remained steady, but Cole knew he was already on very thin ice, 'Just what are you saying, Cole? You're not happy with the way I'm reconstructing this piece of Australian history? Or maybe I'm making them up as I go along?'

Cole took a step towards her, but she turned angrily away and stared out over the tranquil Mary River. Cole walked the few steps to the river's edge keeping a respectful distance between them. He was used to defusing volatile situations and he could not afford to have Sue offside now that they were getting so close to their goal.

He knew he was now in her line of gaze so when he turned around, she was staring directly into his eyes, 'Sue, I honestly love the way you are drawing me into the lives of these people. You are able to show me the events surrounding this plague outbreak through the eyes of individuals. I was just wondering how you know such intimate details about these people.' Cole stood his ground and waited.

Sue took a deep breath, 'These details come from relatives, descendants, crumbling diaries, personal letters and anything that might give me an insight into the lives of these people. You are forgetting that my family has lived here for generations and most of my adult life has been devoted to finding out everything possibly about this plague and the people it killed.'

'I understand.'

'No, Cole, you don't! The O'Connell children died because of neglect, not only from their father but because society at the time considered such filthy, poverty-stricken children to be little more than vermin; a blight on their fair town. Nobody treated them as desperate children in need of help except Mrs. Edwards, Matilda Schafer, Nurse Wiles and Nurse Bauer and they died horribly for their compassion.'

Cole attempted to move a little closer, but Sue put up her hand, 'Just let me say this, Cole. Getting national recognition for these victims is a passion for me.'

Cole moved in and gently placed a hand on her arm, 'Please Sue, I was not questioning your creditability I was just curious as to how you got such detailed information about each person, but I can see it has been a life's work for you. You have intimate information that I would never have been able to find. I truly am grateful.' Cole held out his hand, 'Forgive me?' He smiled one of his rare, dazzling smiles that never failed to catch the recipient off guard. Not so much for their rarity but for the genuine warmth that was fleetingly exposed in his deep green eyes.

Sue tilted her head and gave him a quizzical look before grudgingly accepting his outstretched hand.

'Thank you,' Cole said sincerely. 'May we continue?

Sue smiled and nodded. Cole picked up the story, 'Right

then, it was understandable that the Edwards' family wanted the body to be buried quickly but it is unbelievable that the funeral progressed without a death certificate.'

'Not only that, Cole, but if Doctors Dixon and Penny had been able to perform an autopsy and collect tissue samples for analysis in Brisbane lives may have been saved, especially the nurses. They would at least have known what they were dealing with.'

As they talked Cole was examining the old wharf from every angle. Even hanging over the side to see what lay underneath the blackened planking. He sat up and contemplated the water for a few moments before commenting,' Yes, such a waste. But the mystery remains from where did the pneumonic plague manifest? There is not much of the wharf left here now but I gather this was a large port in its day.' He stood up and dusted his pants then went on to study the road, looking one way then the other as if trying to imagine the site over one hundred years before.

As he still seemed interested in this area Sue filled him in with more details, 'Well, we're lucky to have this much of the wharf left. It was being demolished when residents made such a scream that the council of the day stopped anymore being destroyed and at least this much was preserved. Maryborough was the biggest and busiest port outside of Sydney. Thousands of immigrants arrived here from all over the world. When the immigrant business slackened off the port was essential for the new industries like wool, timber, and sugar. Port Maryborough was even going to be the state's capital at one stage because the river mouth was so wide. That meant that it could handle a large number of ships at one time.'

Cole was now pushing his way through the sturdy scrub growing down the side of the wharf. He seemed to be concentrating on the historic wharf planking, 'So, Sue, the old port was hectic, and bubonic plague was common in most ports around the world. Do you know what precautions were in place to avoid the spread of rats and possible plague here?'

Sue leant over the jetty's side to answer him, 'Actually, they had a pretty good system. For example, any ship tied up to the wharf had to coat its mooring ropes with tar to stop rats climbing down the ropes to the shore. The Harbour Master made inspections of all cargoes and crew for any sign of possible contagious diseases.'

Cole's head disappeared for a few seconds and reappeared on the other side of the wharf. He nodded to Sue to show he was listening as he made his way back to her side, 'Any ship affected by plague or other disease had to place itself in quarantine. They had to display a yellow flag during the day and hang up a red lamp in the evening. Quarantined ships had to remain anchored in the middle of the river and could only communicate with the shore and others ships by signals. Only the health officer was allowed on or off a quarantined ship. Now if you've seen enough here, we'd better head up the hill to visit the Customs House.'

'Sure, just as soon as I have finished this, Sue.'

Cole was writing in his notebook, meticulously recording his findings about the wharf site and next to that the compass readings.

'Oh, right, I forgot about your note taking exercise,' Sue

said over her shoulder as she started up the short hill. 'And before you ask me, this is Macalister Street.'

Sue quickly reached the stately courthouse which had loftily _-presided over its surroundings from the crest of Macalister Street since 1877. She guzzled a few mouthfuls from her water bottle while watching Cole effortlessly lope up the street's incline.

All of a sudden he shot off to the right to investigate some colourful figures overlooking the river. He waved to Sue to join him, 'Can you tell me the purpose of these; what would you call them, statues I suppose?'

'Sure, they're meant to represent a sea captain and a family of immigrants landing in here in 1860. They're made out of old ship's bollards.' It gave Sue an enormous buzz to see that, for once, Cole had no idea what she was talking about.

'Bollards are the big wooden uprights used on ships and docks to tie on the ropes. These figures are facing the mouth of the Mary River and the life they've left behind.'

'How very poetic,' said Cole thoughtfully. 'I can see that this town takes its history seriously.'

Sue gave a slight shrug, 'It's also good for business. While we are here, I want to show you something. In 1905 this road was the same as it is now except it was dirt of course. From here you can see the wharf site, the courthouse and Queens Park. Well, that is the route that Richard O'Connell would have taken to get home after a detour to the pub which was also notorious at the time for the opium den in its basement.' Sue pointed to the old pub still in good repair.

Cole stood on the edge of the road, 'So, you are saying that Richard O'Connell took sacking from the ship's hull and dragged it right past this spot, through the park and straight down the street to his home.'

'That's the story anyway,' replied Sue. 'Can we keep walking? I have to pick the boys up soon from tennis.'
Cole fell into stride with Sue as she powered up the road.

'Now just around that corner,' Sue indicated the direction with a tilt of her water bottle, 'we will come to the Bond Store which was built in 1863 and is now a history museum. But next to that is H.M. Customs House which was built in 1901. Hanging up inside on the right-hand side is a terrific painting of the wharf in its glory days. Just drop a gold coin donation in the box and walk in. I'm going to duck across the road and pick up some cold drinks for the kids. I'll meet you back here in a jiffy, ok?'

Sue was halfway back across the road when Cole emerged from the building. He stood momentarily at the top of the stairs writing in his notations.'

'How was that?' Sue waited at the foot of the stairs.

'Very interesting. Thank you for pointing that out to me.'

'That's ok, I try and think of anything that will help you get a feel for the 1905 era.' Sue was twisting the plastic bag shopping bag around and around her finger and seemed to be reluctant to make eye contact.

'Sue, is there a problem? If I did not know you better, I would say you were nervous.'

'Well, actually Cole, if you don't mind, I'd like your advice on something.'

'Ask away.'

'No, we need to walk up to the next street.'

'Let us walk then but I have to tell you this mysterious persona you have adopted is rather unsettling. You are usually so forthright.'

'Cole, I don't like asking favours but I'm hoping you might understand what I am trying to achieve. Here we are.'

'Well, well, I believe you have brought me to the statue of Mary Poppins. Why?'

'Because if Maryborough can build an elegant statue like this as a tribute to a woman who only lived here for the first few years of her life, then we should build a spectacular monument to honor the lives of two brave nurses, an exceptional good Samaritan and four poor children who might not have died so agonisingly if society had been watching out for them. I've gone so far as sketching out some ideas.'

'Ah, now I begin to see.'

Cole moved to the nearby seat and sat down still studying the statue before him. Sue sat on the edge of the seat next to him. She was watching his face closely, desperately trying to judge his response, 'Cole, aren't the sacrifices of those nurses worth their own statue? I've brought you here because you have seen at first hand the horrific suffering caused by pneumonic plague. You said there was no inoculation available to prevent catching this disease. You said that if patients were not treated within twenty-four hours that the fatality rate is one hundred percent and that some of the areas where this disease breaks out are so isolated that medication arrives too late. This is all correct?

'You are surprisingly correct in every detail. I honestly thought my stories bored you.' Sue shook her head and carried on intently. 'So, knowing that they might fall victim themselves doctors and nurses are still tending pneumonic cases around the world every day, right?'

Cole nodded.

'Then a statue, like the one I'd like for the Maryborough nurses, would also be a public reminder of the continuing sacrifices made by many medical staff around the world. Cole, Australia does not have a good track record for celebrating the achievements and sacrifices of its women. So please, tell me straight, as an impartial observer, do you think I have become obsessed with these victims or is it another example of authorities hiding an unpleasant piece of history from public view?'

Cole stood up and looked at his watch and then looked down into Sue's intent face, 'Sue, I believe in your project more than you will probably understand but we had better start walking or we will be late picking your boys up.'

Side by side they walked briskly back to Cole's car. Sue remained silent, knowing enough about Cole now to realise he was deep in thought. When they reached Cole's car, he unlocked the door for Sue and finally said, 'I believe that your statue idea is a great one, for a number of reasons. Before I leave this town, you will be one of the very few people in this world to fully understand those reasons.'

Sue drew breath to ask a barrage of questions, but Cole shook his head, 'Do not ask me to explain right now. Tomorrow when we meet in front of the Maryborough City Hall you will tell me more about your statue idea. If you bring a copy of your sketches for me, I will use whatever influence I can muster to generate official interest.'

'Thank you for understanding, about the statue I mean.' He gave her a lop-sided grin and added, 'It would be premature to thank me just yet.'

DAY TEN – Obedience and Dedication

JUNE 2, 1905.

"The durability of the Nightingale concept

of the obedient nurse."

Helen Gregory *A Tradition of Care* (1988)

Nurse Rose Wiles awoke with a start. Exhaustion had forced her eyes closed for a few minutes as she sat writing up her notes. Still and heavy was the atmosphere around her. There was no movement, no sound. Nurse Cecelia Bauer was still sitting next to Ritchie O'Connell. Her elbows resting on the bed with her arms outstretched stroking his hands. But now her head was bowed in resignation. She made no utterance, but despair clung over her hunched shoulders like a cloak.

'Cecelia?' Rose called softly.

'Ritchie has gone too, Rose, such a quiet, sincere boy. Tell me Rose, why the doctors can't make these children better. Why must they die so tortuously?' She wasn't crying, which made the scene all the more disturbing.

'Cecelia, you're suffering from exhaustion. While Joanna is in a merciful sleep, I want you to lie down and rest. I will do what is necessary for Ritchie. Doctors can only do so much, but the end result is up to God. And only He knows why events must take a certain course.'

Cecelia was too tired and too depressed to bristle at Rose's unquestionable faith.

*

Doctor Cairns Penny was looking forward to a quite chat with his friend Doctor Lee Garde after the unpleasant events of the day. He gave the office door a cursory knock before letting himself in. Doctor Lee Garde was pedantic about paperwork and was giving his day's notes a final check. He stood up to shake hands when Doctor Penny walked in, 'Good evening, Cairns. You've had a busy day I've been told. Get comfortable before you give me your report. It's rather late; I think we could both use a small sherry?'

Doctor Lee Garde held up a small glass waiting for confirmation, 'I won't say no tonight, Lee. While you and Dixon were talking to the mayor, I went to the train station and collected Doctor Baxter-Tyrie, our government 'plague expert' from Brisbane. His trousers had not had time to warm the seat when he expressed a desire to see the O'Connell home. It is not much of a deviation from the station to the hospital, so I did as he asked. Do you know that without stepping off the buggy he ordered the house to be burned to the ground "plague or no plague" at 3 o'clock tomorrow!

'Yes, I am acutely aware of his orders. He left detailed instructions on my desk. Notify the mayor of this decision, arrange for the fire chief to carry out the burning and contact the police chief to organise keeping curious onlookers at bay.'

Doctor Garde handed Doctor Penny a small sherry, 'Ah, much appreciated, Lee. As you know in the afternoon Doctor Baxter-Tyrie and myself performed a post-mortem examination on young Ritchie O'Connell.'

He reached into his pocket a pulled out a sheet of paper.

These are our official findings. The upper two thirds of the left lung were dark and solid, red hepatisation being well marked. Serosanguineous fluid exuded from cut surfaces. The section sank in water. Several haemorrhagic condensations about the size of a shilling over middle lobe (sic) of left lung. Serosanguineous fluid exuded from mouth and nostril and filled bronchial tubes. Liver large, tough and intensely hyperaemic. No glandular enlargement.' After reading it pushed the sheet of paper towards his friend.

Doctor Garde perused it carefully before commenting, 'It does not appear to be bubonic plague because there has been no glandular swelling in any of the victims. This disease strikes the chest and ultimately the person dies of pneumonia-like symptoms, but they all died in four days. It also appears to be highly contagious which pneumonia is not.' He slowly placed the paper on his desk and smoothed it out while deep in thought, 'Pardon me for stating obvious medical facts; I'm just ruminating aloud, trying to make some sense of it all.' As he spoke he carefully placed a bronze paper weight on the report before he continued, 'And what is Doctor Baxter-Tyrie's expert conclusion?'

Doctor Penny placed his empty glass on the heavy oak desk and shook his head, 'He is of the opinion that Ritchie died of pneumonia. After the post-mortem the viscera were wrapped up and delivered by me personally to Stephen O'Brien, the postmaster. He informed me that the mailbox had been closed for the past fifty-five minutes and that my package was too late for today's mail. I stressed, most persuasively, that it was of the utmost urgency my package left today, and it did. It should arrive in Brisbane early tomorrow.'

Doctor Lee Garde looked a little relieved, 'Good, the results of those samples should tell us with what we are dealing. We do have some excellent news though; two of the O'Connell children have been discharged from the hospital. Kate and May have been sent to the Maryborough Plague Hospital. I do not think they suffer from the same disease as their unfortunate siblings, but we will not take any chances.'

Doctor Cairns Penny lent forward in his chair, 'That is good news indeed and I heard that Matron Tolmie is making a public appeal for clothing for the two girls. All of their clothes, of course, were burned as a precaution when they were admitted to the Maryborough General Hospital.'

'Yes, a fine woman Agnes Tolmie,' stated Doctor Lee Garde. 'She is continually informing me that our nurses are terrified of this disease, but not one has been derelict in her duties.'

Doctor Cairns Penny nodded his tiredly, 'Obedience and dedication, admirable qualities in a nurse. Yes, quite admirable indeed. But now I must be heading off home. We have a big day in front of us and to top it off I have to play peacemaker between two of the most volatile personalities I have ever come across; your half-uncle Doctor Henry Croker Garde and Doctor Baxter-Tyrie.'

'Now that is an explosive combination and not a job I would envy. However, for our friendship's sake, I will attempt to keep H.C. out of the way during Tyrie's presence, if that helps.'

'A true friend indeed, well, till tomorrow then.'

They shook hands and parted company amicably but both men were deeply worried by the mounting body toll and their inability to identify the cause.

PRESENT DAY 10 - JUNE 2.

Cole was listening to Sue as he stared up at the imposing clock tower of the Maryborough City Hall.

'It's a beautiful building, don't you think?' asked Sue.

Cole gave a slight start at the sudden change of subject, 'It has a certain charm about it.'

'It's also proof that Maryborough had a strong social heart at one time,' added Sue as she moved to the shade of a nearby tree.

Cole followed as Sue continued her impromptu history lesson, 'In 1907 Mr. George Ambrose White paid 12,000 pounds to have this built for the people.'

'That was a very generous act for a private citizen, but you are not impressed?' Cole quizzed.

'I think this building is a wonderful testament to Mr. White's generosity. By the time we leave here today you will see why I am not so impressed with the town fathers of the day. But before we get down to the nuts and bolts of all that I'd like to leave by lunchtime if that is ok. My boys are in the inter-school tennis tournament down at Hervey Bay and I'd like to watch them play this arvo.'

'Sure thing, Sue, as soon as you show me your sketches. I presume that is what you are holding under your arm.'

Caught off guard Sue stuttered, 'Well, ah, yes. That is, em you did ask me to bring them.'

Cole held out his hand, 'So, these are your ideas for a statue to honor these nurses of yours?'

Sue kept the folder tucked firmly under her arm, 'Not just the nurses, all of those who died from the pneumonic plague outbreak. Each individual was a tragic story.

'Victims always are, Sue.'

Hesitantly she handed Cole the folder, 'Before you look at these, I'd like to take you around to the side of the city hall. I would like you to understand the whole story of why I'm pushing so hard for this.'

'What more mystery, Sue? Lead the away.'

'Right, well, just around the corner here to the side of the city hall.'

A canopy of densely foliaged branches offered shade over some timber seats near a large, stonewalled fountain. A silvery spray of water spouted from its center and cooled the hot, dusty breeze.

'Cole, I don't know exactly why you are here in Maryborough and I'm damned sure there is more to your "research" than you've told me. But you seem to understand why I want to give Nurse Bauer and Nurse Wiles the national recognition I believe they deserve. May I quickly run through some of my observations on the plague event in 1905?'

'Sure,' said Cole as he stretched out his long legs.

'Once the O'Connell children had been admitted into hospital showing the same symptoms that John O'Connell and Mrs. Edwards had before their deaths the medical superintendent Doctor Lee Garde knew they had a nasty problem. The children needed twenty-four-hour care and had to be kept isolated. It is my opinion that Nurses Bauer and Wiles were handpicked for this job. They needed nurses who did not have an active social life and therefore would be less inclined to spread the disease around town. They needed nurses who would be content to stay at the hospital for the duration of care for the children.'

Cole nodded, 'I can tell you from my own experiences in Africa that when dealing with a contagious outbreak the nurses selected for the job were usually from outlying villages because they had fewer contacts, and as you stated, were less inclined to socialise. So why were these nurses chosen.'

'Well, Nurse Bauer was actually on leave from her hospital duties preparing for her wedding. Nurse Wiles was a responsible and respectable daughter of a Methodist minister. Both came from outside of town. If they were handpicked for this reason, it is even more disgraceful that they have not been suitably acknowledged by the town that summoned them to their deaths.'

Cole folded his legs under the seat and took off his sunglasses to look at Sue, 'Or they just might have been the best nurses for the job? Sue, I have read the notes you gave me, you know. After the event there were some serious accusations made between the Maryborough doctors and the government health officials. But why have you bought me here?'

'In memory of these nurses, no doubt due to the constant pushing by Dr. Earnshaw sixty odd years after their deaths, this fountain was erected in their honour. Matron Tolmie, who was ninety-three years old at the time attended the dedication. She recalled, *"The Maryborough General Hospital nurses were terrified, but not one flinched from doing the duties allotted her during that fateful time."*

'Cole you are sitting in front of the public but belated display of appreciation for those nurses. The town did name the Bauer Wiles Community Health Centre but it is tucked away in Neptune Steet. I was also told there was a Bauer and Wiles Nursing Bursary but have not been able to find out much about that or if it still operating.' Sue put her sketches down on the seat and walked to the fountain. She beckoned Cole to follow her and pointed to the plague set into the stone wall. Although Cole read out the inscription softly and reverently to Sue's ears his foreign accent only accentuated the impersonal nature of these words,

'This fountain was presented to the city by The Maryborough Junior Chamber of Commerce to honour the memory off Nurses Bauer and Wiles who gave their lives nursing the victims of an outbreak of pneumonic plague, "The Black Death" in June 1905. This outbreak was the third recorded in history. Ah, I do see what you mean now, Sue. Certainly, a delayed show of gratitude.'

Cole ran his fingers lightly over the marble inscription as Sue continued, 'Not only that, but it had also been allowed to fall into disrepair until it was cleaned and restored for the centenary, an odd thing for a town so proud of its history.'

'Indeed. Now that you have set the scene may I see your sketches?'

Cole picked the sketches up off the park bench and slowly walked towards the front of the city hall. He deliberated over each one, occasionally glancing out at the city hall green with his head tilted slightly.

'These are very good, Sue. So, you have talent as a sketch artist and a designer.'

'No, I can't take all the credit for the design. A lot of people over the years have had input. I've always been able to sketch a bit, so I was able to put it on paper.'

'I am sure you want to run off now and watch your sons

play tennis,' Cole said as he slipped the sketches back into the folder. 'I should like to keep these to show my contacts just in case they can offer any suggestions.'

'Sure, if you want. They're only copies anyway.'

'Good. We meet up tomorrow, where?'

Sue slung her handbag over her shoulder, 'At the site of the O'Connell home; tomorrow is the burning.

She walked off but Cole touched her lightly on the arm, 'Just a query before you go; the government health officer of the day, Doctor Baxter-Tyrie, seemed determined to play down any discovered cases of plague, firstly the ones in Childers and then the Maryborough cases. Around the world and all through history, when plague is suspected it is announced publicly immediately. This is the first time I have heard of government guys pretending it did not exist. Is it the trade embargo with New South Wales the only reason do you think?'

Sue hesitated for a while before offering, 'Do you mean political intrigue, government cover-ups, that sort of thing?' With a thinly veiled sigh of frustration she added slowly, 'Cole, I really think that is more your line of work. Perhaps you'll tell me before you leave.'

Sue walked off unaware of the integrity issues she'd unleashed in Cole. For a fleeting moment they'd threatened to replace his iron-clad obligation to duty with moral turmoil.

'For God's sake get a grip,' Cole admonished himself, 'in seven days we are out of here, our duty done for the greater good some would say.'

But still he looked back at the fountain with what Sue

considered was a grossly inadequate plaque before his reconnaissance with Chappie and the newly arrived Mortuary Response Team.

DAY ELEVEN – The Burning

JUNE 3, 1905.

'Plague, brought by rats,

prevented by ants; disinfect-ants.'

Australian newspaper advertisement early 1900's.

Doctor Graham Dixon was livid, 'Arson! Legalized or not, it is still arson. Mayor Dawson, this is 1905 not the Middle Ages.'

'Keep your voice down. If we are dealing with plague, it is my duty to protect the citizens.'

Mayor Dawson and Doctor Dixon were standing in the 'Official's Only' cordoned off area on the foot path with a clear but safe view of the proceedings that would soon envelop the O'Connell home. For the sake of decorum Doctor Dixon dropped his voice, a little, 'And what of the O'Connell family, where will they go after this?'

'Be realistic, Graham, of the seven O'Connell children admitted to hospital five are now deceased. It's not good odds that the remains of the family will survive. And the father?' Mayor Dawson answered sympathetically, 'He seems unparticular as to where he sleeps when he's drunk.'

'Which would appear to be quite regularly,' sniffed Doctor Baxter-Tyrie who had walked up behind the arguing men.

'Everyone is painfully aware of your opinions, Doctor Baxter-Tyrie. I believe your exact words were, "burn it down plague or no plague" the instant you saw this unfortunate house,' Doctor Dixon retorted.

'They're coming, they're coming,' chanted nearby children as the surrounding crowd erupted into boisterous cheers and claps.

'Move over, make room,' shouted the grim Superintendent of Police. With his arms outstretched he forced a pathway through the straining necks and eager chatter.

'Make way now! Move over.' Two rows of determined junior officers followed behind, energetically shoving people off the road and back onto the footpath. At the command of their superior the officers formed a human barricade between the over-excited people and the O'Connell home. They stood to attention and glared into the crowd.

Mayor Dawson kept his eyes on these proceedings but leaned over slightly towards his antagonist and whispered firmly, 'Graham, the O'Connell house will be burned down. Accept it as a necessity for community protection.'

'Dear God mayor, this is home for seven motherless children and their father. For three years they've lived like this. Where was your precious 'community protection' for these young citizens?'

Mayor Dawson's wounded reply was drowned out by the applause as the fire trucks approached. Their harnesses glittered in the afternoon sun as the horses hauled the steam engine to its destination. Rather than serve as an imminent warning, the incessant clanging of the fire bell sent a thrill through the crowd until the gleaming horses were almost upon them, forcing people to scatter.

Like a synchronized dance the firemen who'd arrived clinging to the side of a water wagon jumped off and energetically unwound the hose to be used to douse the fire once the deed was done.

Stacked with large asbestos sheets the last wagon drew up.

With precision training the firemen rushed to its side and hauled off the large sheets. They erected them between the O'Connell home and its immediate neighbours. It was hoped that this tactic would prevent stray sparks from setting them alight also. Once satisfied that all was in order, the Superintendent of Police and the Superintendent of the Fire Brigade walked smartly to the official's area to report to the mayor.

'Are you ready to proceed, Mr. Rhule?'

Mr. John David Rhule, the Superintendent of the Fire Brigade, stepped forward, 'Everything is in place, Mayor Dawson.'

'Do your duty then sir,' commanded the mayor.

Mr. Rhule marched to an orderly collection of objects placed next to the cottage. He climbed up a short stepladder placed under a window and bellowed out orders,

'Johnson! Two bags of wood shavings.'

Johnson handed up two hessian bags as Rhule balanced his stomach on the windowsill. He placed the sawdust bags on the floor, 'God Johnson, the stench in here's enough to make you gag.'

To aid in the burn Rhule needed to slit open the hessian bags. He reached one hand behind his back to pull out the pocketknife, the other he placed on the floor to keep his balance. But his hand did not register the hardwood floor; instead, it sank into something soft. He looked down to see a dead grey kitten. This tiny corpse, cold and alone in the filth, seemed to reflect the short, pathetic lives of the O'Connell children, whose days had been a struggle from birth to death. Rhule pushed such sentimental notions from his mind and huskily ordered the kerosene.

Once the fluid had been poured in through the window, he was handed a flaming firebrand to set it alight. Rhule returned to the official party as the room blazed behind him. Johnson had collected the stepladder and loaded it back on the wagon as the short-lived fire waned, flickered and then died into embers. A flurry of hushed conversation rippled through the V.I.P.'s.

With nods all round Mr. Rhule approached the cottage and ordered the same ingredients to be delivered to the opposite window. He repeated the routine of wood shavings, kerosene, and firebrand. A burst of flames looked most promising but all too soon it was also reduced to smoking embers. By now the dignitaries were highly embarrassed and the crowd was fidgety.

One larrikin in the front row nudged his mate in the ribs and yelled out to Superintendent Rhule, 'Makes ya' wonda' don't it, how many homes really go up by accident.'
He was rewarded with an aggressive shove by one of the junior police officers. When the larrikin raised an indigent howl at his unjust treatment the frustrated crowd threatened to turn into an unruly mob.

Rhule made another trip to the V.I.P. section where every form of burning was discussed and evaluated. Eventually the old-fashioned method was voted as the best course of action for this situation.

All firemen were ordered to collect wood from every nearby house and a faggot pile was formed under a corner of the O'Connell home. Then the wood shavings were spread over and around the pile before everything was drenched with kerosene. This time when it was ignited the house went up like a bonfire. Nearly everyone was satisfied. The V.I.P.'s had carried out their civic duty and the townspeople had an event spectacular enough to discuss for weeks.

Only Mr. John Bartholomew, a Melbourne man, had cause for discontent. He was the unfortunate owner of the O'Connell home and his fire insurance policy, *mirabile dictum* (amazing to relate), had been cancelled the day before. This was thought to be a most satisfactory arrangement for everyone except, of course, Mr. John Bartholomew. Before they headed home for dinner the fire brigade doused the smoldering remains of the O'Connell home and their possessions. With nothing left to see the crowd broke up and wandered off to their respective homes.

In the V.I.P. section the mayor waited for his buggy to be returned to him. All the buggies of the dignitaries and doctors had been driven to a makeshift compound at the end of the road once their very important masters had alighted. It was feared that these highly-strung and often skittish show ponies might take fright at the sight and smell of the fire. When his buggy arrived, Mayor Dawson was accompanied home by Doctor Baxter-Tyrie. Together they trotted off without a second glance at the desolation that had been created.

Doctor Dixon stood next to the burnt rubble of the children's home when Doctor Lee Garde gave him a light pat on the back. Doctor Dixon looked at his friend sadly,

'At least the Edwards home was fumigated and only Lettie's clothing and bedding was burned. But all this pitiable family had was a roof over their heads and we destroyed even that.'

'It's a sad business, Graham, but my word you gave the

mayor quite a speech.'

'Well Lee, your pay cheque is signed by the State Government, Robinson's too, Doctor Baxter-Tyrie is the State Government representative and therefore it would not be prudent for any of you to engage in public criticisms, had you the desire to do so. As I am a free agent, I felt obliged to say my piece. Ah, there is Penny. Excuse me a moment while I call him over. Doctor Penny, please join us.'

Doctor Penny was striding down the centre of the road but stopped when he heard his name. He gave a quick wave of acknowledgment and retraced his steps to greet them, 'I wasn't being rude I thought you may have been in deep discussions considering the events of the day.'

Doctor Dixon reassured him, 'It is for precisely that reason why I called you over. While there is no one else about I would like to discuss the Doctor Baxter-Tyrie problem.'

'Do you mind if we walk at the same time? I put my new thoroughbred in harness this morning not realising it was going to be such a long day. He just might be getting unsettled by now. He has been rigged up since I was called out this morning to assist Doctor Baxter-Tyrie with the autopsy on Johanna O'Connell. Poor child, lovely red hair you know.'

'Yes, a tragic business. I'm sorry Penny, I only had time for a quick glance at your report this morning, just enough to make sure Johanna died of the same disease as the other children. I then spent the day trying to convince Doctor Baxter-Tyrie that we have a plague incident. Have you noticed how unusually reticent he and the mayor are in accepting our diagnoses? Doctor Penny, would you mind going over your findings again?'

'Not at all. The lower lobe of her left lung was found to be in a state of red hepatisation with recent pleurisy over the affected area. She had no glandular enlargements.'

Doctor Lee Garde was pensive for a moment, 'Just like the others. Are you both aware that Nurse Bauer is now desperately ill? I had her family notified today and they will be visiting tomorrow.'

Doctor Dixon was a little surprised, 'You're so certain she will not recover?'

Doctor Lee Garde shook his head slowly, 'It is unlikely. Let's hope Brisbane notifies us soon about those test results. We must know for certain what we are dealing with. Doctor Baxter-Tyrie has now had the hospital ward quarantined and ordered all the contents burned. I will be submitting a requisition to the Health Department *posthaste* for the replacement of the destroyed property.'

Everyone nodded in agreement as they reached their respective buggies. Doctor Penny inquired tiredly, 'Talking of Doctor Baxter-Tyrie where was Doctor H.C. Garde today? I was waiting for the eruption.'

Doctor Lee Garde answered, 'Someone had to man the hospital. He was reasonable on that matter. But be warned, a clash between those two is imminent and we will all be forced to show our colours as you would say Penny.'

Doctor Penny's magnificent thoroughbred was fidgety, as he'd predicted. Police cadets, acting as stable boys for the afternoon, were relieved to hand over the last of their charges and go home. Bidding each other a somber good night, the doctors turned their horses towards home. By seven pm the street was deserted.

PRESENT DAY 11 - JUNE 3.

Cole was snapped back into the modern world by the disorientating noise of a bell clanging nearby. So deeply engrossed was he in reliving the destruction of the O'Connell hut that he'd almost expected to see the fire brigade drawing near with its warning bell ringing instead of the local ice-cream van gliding past.

Sue had excelled herself with her description of the events that surrounded the burning. So, moving was her story that, although she had left an hour ago, her words were still resonating through Cole's head as he waited for Chappie. Slowly the ice-cream van continued down the street trolling for business as a dark green jeep pulled up next to Cole.

A khaki clad driver nodded respectfully to him. Chappie was sitting in the passenger side and handed over a file, 'A list of the Mortuary Response Team.'

'Any fresh new faces,' Cole asked as he ran his eyes down the list.'

'Not really,' answered Chappie. 'Most are straight from our Montpellier digs in France.'

Cole nodded, 'That mass grave outside Montpellier was full of possible plague victims from the 13th and 14th century. We have to know for sure if it was plague that killed those millions of people; and if so, was it the same strain we are threatened with today. Deiter and his team were going to subject the human remnants to the new Suicide DNA technique. Did anything conclusive come out of that?

Cole handed the file back to Chappie who locked it in the glove compartment, 'Ah, a whole can of worms there, Cole. Deiter is setting up his gear at the cemetery and will no doubt go into infinite detail for you. But in a nutshell, they extracted some good DNA from the tooth pulp of four skulls. Some of the tests showed plague DNA but it depends on which 'expert' you talk to apparently, so controversy is now raging in some heavy weight international quarters.'

Chappie unfolded his large frame out of the jeep and had an enormous stretch. Cole shook his head slightly, 'That is a shame. It might have hastened our time here. We no longer have the luxury of excess days.'

Cole motioned to the driver who put the jeep in gear and drove off leaving a cloud of brown dust to linger for a moment. As they walked towards Cole's four-wheel drive Chappie gave a quick progress report, 'Well, you'll be pleased to know that all the vans have arrived and are at the cemetery site now.'

'Any problems from the authorities?' queried Cole.

Chappie gave a quick laugh before answering, 'No, the official story is we are part of a Queensland Government project to preserve the sunny state's past by restoring its historic cemetery. It's fortunate for us that Maryborough played such an important role in this state's history.

Local police will barricade the road tomorrow and the work will start on restoring and cleaning the gravestones for real. After a few days of that the public and the media should have covered the story and leave us alone.'

Cole jumped in behind the steering wheel, 'And the biosphere?'

Chappie hauled his tall frame into the passenger side as he grunted, 'Brand new one flying in as we speak. Guaranteed untainted so our DNA harvest will be as pure as humanly possible. Inflation will start 2400 on day sixteen.'

Cole started the engine but then turned toward his friend. His face betrayed no emotion, 'It will remain inflated for twenty-four hours precisely and then it and us will be gone. I am making it your responsibility to ensure that Deiter and the Mortuary Response Team get every bit of DNA sample they need from the pneumonic plague victims within that time frame. Is that understood Chappie?'

Chappie answered with equal seriousness, 'You know it'll be done. Now, securing the perimeter, what tactic do you want to use?'

Cole hit the accelerator and spun the wheels in the dirt before the tyres gripped the bitumen. As they roared up the road towards the cemetery he continued, 'All of our men will be on the gravesites restoration duty so we will have plenty of backup just in case we get some overzealous onlookers. Once the bio-spere is up I want every man on twenty-four-hour armed guard until that tent is down.'

'What?' Chappie shot out. 'If we show arms we've got to be in full uniform.'

'That is affirmative but at all times weapons will be held at the reverse arms position as a visual sign of mourning and respect. At absolutely no time under any circumstances are weapons to be displayed other than in reverse arms position. Am I clear, Chappie?'

Chappie was about to question this decision further when Cole cut him short, 'Now on a lighter note, my friend, I have a question for you. Something Sue taught me.'

'You two have a lot of fun on these daily jaunts, don't you?'

Cole ignored his friend's deliberate taunt, 'You love Latin so much, tell me what 'mirabile dictu' means.'

'Come on Cole, I only know church Latin and a smattering of ancient Roman. But I can tell by that smug look that you know. So, spill, what does 'mirabile dictu' mean?

'It was used, even in the newspapers here, to introduce something genuinely or ironically amazing. I am told it comes from the Latin words 'amazing to relate'.

Chappie laughed, 'Well, well the things you pick up in this job. Thanks for that, I'm sure I'll be able to casually drop it into a conversation sometime. But all joking aside Cole what are you going to do when Sue finds out you've dug up her nurses to collect DNA samples?'

'With any luck she will not know until it is all over. If I am not that lucky then we can expect a very big explosion. One more thing Chappie, and this is a priority order, no one is to challenge or detain Sue no matter where she is.'

'Even the cemetery, Cole?'

'Especially the cemetery! Sue and I are not meeting up tomorrow. I need to get things organized before that biosphere arrives, but we can expect a ferocious reaction when Sue sees what we are doing. Have me notified as soon as she roars up to the cemetery gates. I will handle her my own way.'

DAY THIRTEEN – Goodbyes

JUNE 5, 1905.

"We express our endless gratitude to the Chinese people,

and our deepest apologies."

Yoshio Shinozuka Unit 731.

'Cecelia dear, can you sit up for me? Your family will be here soon to visit.'

Cecelia became wild eyed and frantic, 'Don't let them in, Rose. Don't let them. Oh God.'

She folded her arms across her chest and rocked backwards and forwards coughing. Rose held her shoulders and comforted her. She stroked her hair and soothed her concerns, 'Don't fret, dear. We will keep away from the doors, but your family will be able to see you through the glass.'

Her coughing had finished but it left her breathless and wheezing. Talking, without pacing her breaths, was becoming increasingly difficult, 'Rose, do the doctors know what it is yet?'

'Doctor Lee Garde came by yesterday when you were sleeping. He will get Doctor Penny to chase up Brisbane for the results of those autopsy samples. But right now, we must get you looking nice for your family. For the moment you are my patient, and I want you to save your strength. Let me do everything. First, we will have a sponge bath and then we will put on a clean uniform.'

Once Cecelia was dressed and her hair neatly pinned up under her cap Nurse Wiles helped her into a wheelchair chatting cheerily, 'Nurse Sprague will let us know when your visitors are nearly here. Then I will wheel you closer to the doors and leave the wheelchair under the glass section. Your family will not be able to see it but you can hold onto it for support. How does that sound?'

'Rose what will I say to them? They'll be so worried.'

'Tell them you have your very own nurse, and the doctors are doing everything in their power to cure you.'

She looked up to see Nurse Sprague signaling her through the round glass on the top half of the ward doors.

'Here come your parents. Ready? Up you get then.'

Annie and Felix Bauer gently touched the glass that separated them from their beautiful, pale daughter. She was standing inside her ward and smiled when she saw them. Anne choked back the raw emotion that might have overwhelmed her. Now was not the time. Calm and love. Calm and love. That was all they could give her. She took in a few deep breaths, allowing her husband to open the conversation.

'Celi pup, these doctor's looking after you all right?'

Capable and self-reliant Felix was not good at small talk. He had not called his daughter by her nickname 'Celi pup' since she was a toddler spending her days rolling in the grass with the regular broods of puppies produced by the working dogs. In those days she was as plump and as round and as playful as any pup. So, the name stuck.

In those days too he could fix any problem that brought tears to his little girl's eyes. But in the face of this disease he could not waste what little time they had left in lamentations.

Annie had composed herself and started chatting; the sugar yield might be high this year, the Guernsey milking cow had a Friesian calf, don't know how that could have happened, the young colt is nearly ready to break in, what was that tip again to make the Lilli Pilli jam set properly, Mrs. Hynes's baby had his first tooth.

Felix watched powerlessly as Cecelia's strength faded before his eyes. He nudged Anne who wrapped up the casual tête-à-tête in a natural manner. She put her hand up to glass and spread her fingers wide, 'Darling, we love you. Please rest and get well.'

Cecelia nodded. She didn't want to cry and risk a distressing cough fit in front of her parents. She swallowed hard and took some deep breaths. Willing herself to keep calm. Felix tried to look relaxed as he rubbed his hands together and announced in his matter-of-fact father's voice, 'Celi pup. We'll be back tomorrow. Here's Will to see you now. Bye, love.'

'Will could see the strain was almost too much for his fiancée. She was trembling and obviously holding onto something. Rose came to her side and held her shoulders. For a silent moment Cecelia studied his handsome features. A flash of the life she was not going to have rushed through her mind, her beautiful wedding dress, their romantic honeymoon, decorating their new home and some angelic babies. She felt sorry for the pain her passing would cause. Her large, gentle eyes were tormented with sadness and finality. She knew she would be dead before their next meeting.

'I'm so sorry, Will,' was all she could say before a swirl of darkness threatened to engulf her.

'Get better Celi, please get better!'

But Cecelia had slumped into the wheelchair and Rose was

pushing her towards the bed. His strong tanned hands trembled as he turned to follow the stooping figures of his fiancée's parents. They would need his strength soon. There was nothing he could do for their daughter now.

Nurse Sprague waited until the sad group had left then tapped on the doors, 'Nurse Wiles, may I speak to you a moment?'
Rose was gently laying Cecelia on the bed, 'Yes, Nurse Sprague.'

'I thought you should know that Doctor Ham has ordered two nurses from the Brisbane Plague Hospital to come here and help. Doctor Penny said they were very experienced in caring for plague victims. They will be arriving by train today.'
Cecelia was alarmed and tried to speak in between coughing bouts, 'No, Rose, they mustn't! It spreads so quickly.'

'Cecelia is right. Until they know what disease is inflicting this town nobody should come near us added Rose.
'But Nurse Wiles you're exhausted. You and Cecelia have shouldered the burden of this outbreak. Shouldn't you have a rest and let someone look after you?'

'We can discuss this later but thank you for keeping us informed.'
Nurse Sprague left to report to Matron and Rose returned to her friend's side.

Cecelia was getting weaker by the minute. As Rose deftly changed Cecelia's uniform for her nightdress, she could feel the burning heat emanating from her skin. For the rest of the day and all through the night Rose attended to her friend. Cecelia's temperature was soaring, and she was slipping in and out of delirium. Her mild cough was now choking and persistent. The thin watery sputum had become thick, and blood stained. Rose knew her loving and dedicated friend was living out her last few torturous hours.

*

At the same time a crowd of nurses and wards men had gathered outside the office doorway of Doctor Lee Garde. A serious confrontation was brewing between Doctor Charles Baxter-Tyrie and Doctor Henry Croker Garde, who had both unfortunately decided to visit the Hospital Superintendent at the same time. Their obstinate arguing could be heard down the length of the hallway. Matron Tolmie pushed her way none too gently through the giggling crowd.

'What a disgraceful show of disregard for the professionalism of your post. Return to work this instant. And you, Sister, fetch Doctor Lee Garde immediately!'

'No need thank you matron, my hearing is quite adequate enough to pick up those voices from down at the surgery H.C. has never been one to hold his tongue, no matter what the circumstances, or how high was the official position of the unfortunate recipient of his opinion.'

A confrontation which had started with just raised voices was quickly deteriorating into furious bursts of exchanged insults.

'Blast you Tyrie, as our so-called plague expert' you should have done your job thoroughly and bought your microscope with you. A simple examination of the sputum would have revealed the large numbers of plague bacilli. I will quote Doctor Burnett Ham, "In the cases of plague without external buboes but with pneumonic symptoms a bacteriological examination is the only accurate way to determine this disease." I put it to you Tyrie that one or more of these children would still be alive if you had carried your scientific microscope with you.'

If the office door had been open the audience outside would have seen Doctor Baxter-Tyrie's eyes blazing in temper as he boomed out his reply, 'It is an outrageous state of affairs that a hospital of this size does not have its own powerful microscope. That child's toy stored at the School of Arts is totally useless for medical analysis of this nature.' Doctor Baxter-Tyrie practically sneered his next comments. 'Apparently you are not aware of the fact that bacilli cannot be detected with the ordinary lens of the average microscope. For bacterioscopic examination a somewhat expensive oil immersion objective is absolutely necessary, and none such was available in Maryborough. If the microscope at the School of Arts were sufficient for the purpose, why did not the Medical Superintendent of the Hospital, Doctor Lee Garde, examine the sputum himself before I arrived?'

Doctor H.C. Garde was not going to let this insult go unattended, 'Why did you not telegraph on Friday afternoon for your own microscope then? It could have been here by 6 a.m. the next day.'

Now that the crowd around the door had dissipated with stern encouragement from Matron Tomlie, Doctor Lee Garde entered his office in a congenital manner and attempted to douse the flames of ill temper with professional calmness. But his appearance caused Doctor H.C. Garde to appeal to him as an ally, 'Ah, Lee, good man, you heard this lunatic when he arrived. We have no plague; he stated it categorically. Why he even laughed at the idea. He is either mad or grossly incompetent!'

Doctor H.C. Garde was beyond blustering and quite capable of resorting to fisticuffs if all else failed. Doctor Lee Garde stood his ground between them. He spoke softly but firmly so that they had to quieten down and stop pacing around each other if they were to hear his words, 'H.C.,' Doctor Lee Garde gave him a stern look before turning his head to address his other visitor, 'Doctor Baxter-Tyrie, the behavior of you both as medical men is contemptible. You have made my office a three-ring circus of entertainment for the staff while Nurse Cecelia Bauer fights for her life. Until I get answers on how to defeat this disease neither of you will be welcome back into my office. Any complaints you have against each other put in writing and send to Doctor Burnett Ham. Let him deal with you.'

Doctor Lee Garde sat down behind his desk, 'Both of you will leave immediately and get back to your work.'

Doctor H.C. Garde, for all his fiery temper, knew that Lee was right and headed for the door, but Doctor Baxter-Tyrie was beside himself with indignation at being dismissed.

He glared at Lee before exploding with, 'How dare you! Just who do you think you are talking to?'

Doctor Lee Garde stood up and firmly placed his hands on his desk and leaned forward,

'I am talking to a government representative who appears to spend more time engaged in arguments with eminent local surgeons than diagnosing this epidemic.'

Doctor Baxter-Tyrie took a step back, 'Now, now it is hardly an epidemic.'

'It will be if you don't do your job. Come back when you have some answers for me.'

As Doctor Baxter-Tyrie headed towards the closed door he could have sworn that he heard Doctor H.C. Garde chuckling on the other side but when he stepped out into the hallway it was empty. No matter, he thought, he'd be filing his complaints against these hick doctors immediately on his arrival back in Brisbane.

PRESENT DAY 13 - JUNE 5.

Cole and Sue were again sitting under the spreading branches of the red flowering Poinciana tree in front of the plague ward of the old hospital. Her last few words seemed to hang heavily in the air. Cole was preoccupied and Sue knew now it was better to leave him alone until he was ready to talk.

Eventually he seemed to make a decision and was intent on acting on it, 'Sue, I have read all of your notes and newspaper clippings and I want you to know that no matter what might occur in the next few days to make you think otherwise, I sincerely believe in your desire to give the nurses and the other victims the recognition they deserve.'

'Why are you talking like that, Cole? You are going to do something I won't approve of, is that it? Why should it bother you what I think?'

Cole stood up and took both her hands in his, 'Sue, my mobile office is still here in the hospital driveway. Are you prepared for some very disturbing information about the pneumonic plague and why I am here?'

She frowned at him suspiciously.

'Sue, I am trying to understand your cause so will you at least attempt to understand mine?'

'But won't that go against whatever regulations you are working under?'

Looking directly into her eyes he stated simply, 'Yes, it will.'

He let go of her hands and walked to the white caravan. Two men in khaki shirts and shorts standing at either end of the caravan nodded as Cole approached. They walked smartly off five meters in either direction but remained watchful. Sue came up beside him, 'I'm not going to like any of this am I?'

'No, but it will give you a glimpse into my world.'
Inside the caravan Sue was surprised to see the walls were covered in posters and photos of the most pristine areas on the planet. Cole noted her gaze, 'They are to keep us motivated; to remind us that the world is worth saving. Please sit down in front of the computer.

Now, you have heard the term 'germ warfare' and 'biological weapons' I'm sure many times on television. These words refer to the technique of using living microorganisms such as plague bacteria to wipe out a population while leaving the buildings and industries intact. Our research found the first recorded case of such an action was in 1346 when the Tartars catapulted plague-ridden corpses into the city of Kafka.'

'That's horrible. Cole, I really don't think I want to hear or see any more.'
Cole was standing behind her as he narrated the slide show appearing before her. Until now his voice had remained matter of fact, but he hesitated for a moment and then almost pleaded, 'Please Sue, it is extremely important to me that you understand just a little of what I need to do.'

'I'm trusting you on this one, Cole. I'll stay if you really think it is important.

'More than that Sue, it is imperative!'
Sue looked up at the posters and slowly nodded.

'Thank you, Sue. I have told you that part of my job is to study outbreaks of pneumonic plague around the globe and through history. Why is this information so important?

Because it can be used as an effective weapon. I will share with you some information on how the plague virus has been used as a weapon in the most documented series of events that we have on hand today.

In 1925 Japan refused the Geneva Convention ban on biological weapons. By 1936 the Japanese had invaded northern China and the infamous 'UNIT 731' had been formed. Doctor Shiro Ishi was an army officer and a physician intrigued by the possibility of using diseases as weapons. He began preliminary experiments using the local Chinese population as subjects or 'logs' as they called them. It is recorded that tens of thousands died after the dropping of 'plague bombs' and the releasing of plague infected animals to wipe out villages. During the final days of the Pacific war in 1945 they blew up UNIT 731 and any subjects still alive to cover up their experiments.

In 1946 the United States made a deal with Doctor Ishi in exchange for immunity from war-crimes prosecution he surrendered all of the findings from his experiments.'

Sue's hands were shaking as she reluctantly watched the photos Cole presented to her on the screen. Each image of the dead and dying was more disturbing and horrifying than the one before it.

'I'm sorry Cole I don't know if this is true or just a scare tactic or even a conspiracy theory, but I can't believe that any democratic society would make a deal like that if someone did such awful things, even if it was war. It's horrible.'

'I have seen the evidence with my own eyes. I have read the official war files and studied Ishi's notes. It happened. You can search all this on the net.'

He sat next to Sue but did not look in her direction. When he spoke, his voice was so chillingly emotionless that it forced a shiver to ripple up and down her spine.

'I can tell you one thing for nothing, Sue, I have not even touched on the true horror of Unit 731. It would be far too much for you. Just remember that I am dealing with this every day.'

In a whirlwind change of disposition, which she'd come to accept as a Cole characteristic, he slapped his knees and stood up, 'Perhaps it might explain my 'bloody man-moods as I have heard you say under your breath when you believe I am being difficult or eccentric.'

'Well, maybe I should apologize for that but if I must hear this story then let's get to the end quickly, please.'

'Certainly, Imperial Japan was tenacious in its belief that world domination could be had by the use of plague bacteria. They were experimenting with sending thousands of hot air balloons full of plague infected fleas across the Pacific on the jet stream to America.

Except for the end of the war probably the most successful would have been the mission codenamed by Doctor Ishi himself as 'Cherry Blossoms at Night. Kamikaze pilots were to drop plague bombs over California to infest towns, water supplies and livestock. They would be taken close to the coastline in Japan's newly designed I-400 giant submarines especially designed to carry three-fold-wing planes. They could quickly surface in the open sea, launch the planes and submerge before being detected. Had this plan succeeded it would have stretched the American medical resources to breaking point.

And to finish off with I will just add one note for you to

consider. Biological warfare programs are reported to still be underway by numerous unfriendly countries. A few sketchy communications we have received from our field teams indicate that a strain of 'super plague' has been developed which responds to no known treatment. And that,' Cole turned off the computer, 'is my day job.'

Sue watched silently as the images dissolved into dots then disappeared. She stood up slowly and walked to the door. Cole softly called after her, 'Sue, there is only one thing I need you to remember.'

'And that is?' she asked flatly as she hesitated in the doorway.

'Just remember that no matter what, I have the highest of respect for your nurses and what you are trying to achieve. I know you do not understand at the moment, but I am helping you as much as I am able.'

'Yea? Well, I'll just keep that in mind.'

Cole took her gently by the elbow and guided her in the direction of her car. As they passed the two khaki clad men Cole gave them a nod. They moved back to the caravan and after locking it securely took up their positions.

'Sue, I know that what you have seen is a shock. We all felt like that the first time we were exposed to it, but I only have a few days left here. What you have just seen is what I am trying to prevent from occurring again. Please say you will continue with your plague story tomorrow for me?'

'I suppose so Cole, if you are truly interested.'

'Sue, I will be in your debt. Now hand me your keys and I will chauffeur you home. No, no argument. Chappie will pick me up. You sit back and relax. And Sue, well, just thank you.'

DAY FOURTEEN – Diagnosis Pneumonic Plague

JUNE 6, 1905.

'Plague, the pestilence which walketh in darkness,

and the destruction that wasteth at noonday.'

Psalms 91 *Holman Christian Standard Bible*

'Doctor Garde,' Matron Tolmie announced from the doorway, 'the Colmslie Plague nurses have arrived from Brisbane.'

'Good. Show them to the isolation ward.'

Matron remained positioned in the doorway of Doctor Lee Garde's office, 'I have already escorted them to the isolation ward doctor, but our nurses are refusing any help.'

Doctor Lee Garde looked up from his writing, 'Refusing? That is preposterous.'

'Nurse Bauer and Nurse Wiles have refused to go to the train station with the Colmslie nurses. They insist that they will not be transported to the Brisbane Plague Hospital.'

'But those plague nurses are in demand around Australia. They are experienced in dealing with plague patients. What is all this nonsense about?

'Doctor Garde, Nurse Bauer deteriorated greatly throughout the night. No attention or kindness can save her now. Nurse Wiles has exhibited the first signs of contracting the same malady. She was emphatic that they would not be responsible for carrying such a contagious and torturous disease into the capital city. When I approached the isolation ward with the plague nurses Rose pleaded with them to stay away. Her exact words were, "at least until it is known what terrible disease we are dealing with." Cecelia, although slipping in and out of delirium, was lucid enough to weakly wave them away.'

'Thank you, Matron Tomlie. Tell the plague nurses to monitor the condition of our nurses as best they can. We expect the results of the samples to come back today.'

Unexpectedly Doctor Penny strode up to the office doorway and boomed, 'Ah, Garde. Just the man for whom I was searching.'

Matron just had time to step out of his way before he sailed into the office imposing as always in his spotless white uniform, 'Good Lord, I just ran into those plague nurses from Brisbane. Have you seen the garb they wear? The sight of 'em would scare you into your grave. But, that aside I must relay some more bad news. There is a nurse on her way here now to inform matron that your Nurse Cecelia Bauer has just died. That makes seven victims who have died after direct contact with each other.'

Doctor Lee Garde was visibly upset at this latest development but immediately decided on a plan of action, 'Matron Tomlie, have notices put up around the grounds that quarantine is now imposed on the entire hospital. No unauthorized persons are to be permitted on hospital grounds for any purpose. Have the plague nurses remove the body to the morgue. They have all the protective clothing, and they have been inoculated, as we all will be shortly. Assure Nurse Wiles that she will not have to travel to Brisbane and ask her to accept the care of the plague nurses. But first of all, have Nurse Wiles inoculated with twenty cc's of Yersin's Serum, it just might prevent another death.'

Matron Tolmie quickly reentered the office announcing,

'Doctor Garde, I have just been informed that the daughter

of a local shop owner, a Miss Copp, is exhibiting signs of this disease.'

'Have her sent directly to the temporary plague depot in town and get her inoculated quickly.' Doctor Garde ordered. When matron left the room Doctor Penny resumed his announcements, 'I am also the bearer of further news, I am afraid. Doctor Wilson Love will be arriving by train from Brisbane this afternoon. He will be carrying the test results on his person.'

'Is it so bad that we need the President of the Central Board of Health to tell us in person Penny, why not send a telegram?'

'I believe the government is trying to avoid a public panic. Doctor Love is also the Honorary Government Pathologist, and I am privy to the fact that before he left Brisbane this morning, he was in consultation with Doctor Burnett Ham and the Premier of Queensland. I have been notified that Doctor Love has been ordered here to confer with me. I should also mention that Doctor Baxter-Tyrie has received a wire from the Premier's office instructing him to take the necessary precautions.'

Doctor Lee Garde concentrated on his pen trying to place a face to Doctor Love's name as he pondered aloud,

'Whatever affliction these people are dying from the government is now taking an abnormally keen interest.'
Doctor Lee Garde put down the pen as the elusive details flowed back, 'If my memory serves me correctly Doctor Love is a very serene and courteous fellow with the 'turned' right eye. The result of an early childhood accident I understand.'
Doctor Penny nodded cautiously, 'Your memory is

accurate, but it would be prudent to remember how sensitive Doctor Love is about his infliction. Why even in a group shot he will only be photographed on his good side.'

'I shall keep that in mind. So now we have to deal with another Brisbane 'expert' and Doctor Tyrie ready to usurp my authority when all we need are those damn tissue results. H.C. is going to be blazing about this.'

*

At the mayor's office Doctor Crawford Robinson was responding to a personal invitation from Mayor Dawson to visit upon his chamber. Doctor Robinson rapped gently on the door and was rewarded by a rumbled, 'That you, Robinson?'

'Yes, Mayor Dawson,' Doctor Robinson was a little apprehensive.

'Come in man, come in. Close the door and take a seat.'
As Doctor Robinson sat down and waited, he noted that the mayor's face was much more florid than usual. He was also sweating profusely. He seemed highly agitated and without making eye contact with his guest Mayor Dawson thrust towards him a medical report,

'This came today with Doctor Love from Brisbane. It's only taken four- and-one-half days.'
Doctor Robinson read it out aloud, 'Specimen Results. The bacteriological examination of the sections of viscera taken from the body of Ritchie O'Connell revealed numerous *Bacilli pestis* in lungs, liver, spleen, kidneys and heart.'

'This is a bloody disaster, Robinson. Doctor Ashburton Thompson, the president of the New South Wales Board of

Health, is meeting with Doctor Burnett Ham and Premier Morgan in Brisbane today! Do you know what the agenda is to be? The proposed removal of the plague restrictions on Queensland produce. Bankruptcy or survival for thousands of Queensland farmers will be determined by today's decision. New South Wales closed its borders to Queensland goods because of bubonic plague. Do you think they'll reopen it when they hear of this?'

'That is unfortunate mayor, but this report means that we are dealing with the deadliest and most highly infectious of all plagues. Even an inoculation with Yersin's Serum is utterly useless against pneumonic plague. Millions of people died from the Black Plague right across Europe in 1666. And that was just one outbreak. It is capable of wiping out whole towns, even cities!'

Mayor Dawson's red face was pumping out sweat as he paced around and around his desk, 'Where the hell has this come from? How can it just appear from nowhere? But more importantly, Doctor Robinson, can we contain it?'

'Well, the rat catchers have been placed under the direct command of the Inspector for Health. Doctor Baxter-Tyrie and your council officers have made a close inspection of known rat infestations around the city such as butchers and produce stores. The townspeople are diligently searching for and destroying rats and mice. There's been a smoky haze over the town for days from people burning rubbish and rat carcasses. If we can contain the outbreak, then all this activity should lessen the possibility of recurrence. But as no infected rats have been found we are at a loss as to how it started.

'I don't mind telling you Robinson that for a number of

reasons this could not happen at a worse time.

'The plague restrictions you mean?' asked Doctor Robinson reached for a jug of water sitting on the desk and filled a glass. He handed it to Mayor Dawson who gulped it down and placed the glass back on the desk, hardly missing a beat in the conversation.

'Not just the plague restrictions. Our town is suffering enough as it is now the powers-that-be are talking about banning the importation of opium. That will leave Maryborough with thousands of desperate addicts, mainly Chinese and blacks. There'll be big trouble, you mark my words. And the loss of Customs Tax doesn't bear thinking about. I also have the Reverend J. Thompson making public complaints about the deportation of the Kanakas. "Inhuman and cowardice" he has called it. Why, for trying to send these poor fellows back home? And now I have the Protector of Aborigines, Archibald Meston, stating to anyone who'll listen that "the exceptionally fine race of Aboriginal people on Fraser Island has diminished to approximately twenty from three thousand." I am not sure yet what his expectations are of me to correct this, but I am sure he will submit something.'

'I think you'll find mayor that, as far as this epidemic at least is concerned, every measure available is being taken to ensure this disease is contained. There should be no new cases.'

'My God, I just hope you are right Doctor Robinson.'

PRESENT DAY 14 - JUNE 6.

Sue and Cole were back on the hospital grounds sitting under the branches of the Poinciana tree. Cole breathed in the crisp autumn morning air. This was the last time they would meet here. In front of them stood the grand old hospital building with its ornate trims and shady verandahs. Cole's mobile office caravan had been re-located to the cemetery in preparation for the final stages of his mission.

Sue was animated when recounting her story but was distant to Cole personally. She might be cool now, Cole thought, but she will be after me with all guns blazing in forty-eight hours. Aloud he said warmly, 'Thank you, Sue. You are a true professional to come here today and continue with your nurses' story. I really am grateful.'

'Yea, well, it's a story that should be better known. Maybe something will come out of all this. Look, I'm sorry if I'm a bit off today. I'm still trying to digest what you told me yesterday. I know you had to but still . . .

'Sue believe me, you have no need to apologise. Now let us change the subject? I must make arrangements with you for the next few days. My schedule is becoming drastically tighter.'

'OK, our next meeting should be at the graveside of Nurse Cecelia Bauer. You have my map of its exact location in the cemetery, but I want us to start at the front gates.'
Cole had been staring at the horizon in a preoccupied manner when he drawled, 'That sounds just fine, Sue.'

'Are you ok? You've gone all mysterious again. You enjoy this cloak and dagger stuff, don't you?
Now used to his mood changes Sue turned towards her car

but with lightning speed Cole grabbed her arm and held her still for a moment. He faced her squarely with emotions bared uncharacteristically across his bronzed face, 'Sue, what I am about to do will save millions of lives, but I surely fear that you will hate me.'

He drew his face so close his hot breath warmed her cheek. She was shocked to realize that she was holding her breath as his voice trembled with emotion leaving her in no doubt of the genuine nature of his words, 'I admire you for your attempts at gaining recognition for your nurses. No matter what you might see in the next few days remember . . .' he softly squeezed her shoulders, 'please remember that respect for those nurses will be my highest priority.'

His voice gradually lost its intensity as he looked down at Sue stricken face. He let her go slowly, 'I am sorry I shocked you but I am running out of time. We will meet again tomorrow at the cemetery, yes?'

Sue nodded. Did she detect a hint of sadness in his parting word? He's such a queer cove at times it was hard to know, she thought to herself as she watched him stride away.

DAY FIFTEEN – A White Rose and Wildflowers

JUNE 7, 1905.

'Although my breathing ceases time and tide go on.'

Atsujin (1836)

''ere it is, Funeral Notice,' the gravedigger Harry Hansen read aloud to his labouring offsiders, 'the friends of the late Nurse Cecelia Elizabeth Bauer, aged twenty-two years and one month, of the Maryborough Hospital and beloved daughter of Felix and Annie Bauer of Blackmount Tiaro, are requested to attend her funeral to leave the hospital entrance Walker Street this afternoon at two- forty-five o'clock. J. Ammenhauser, Funeral Director, Adelaide Street. I tells ya' it's gonna' be a big do. A real good payer too I should think.'

'Not for you if you don't get back to work!'
Harry jumped to his feet,

'Mr. Ammenhauser, sir, what are ya' doin here so early? Funerals not fa' hours yet?

'Harry Hansen, because you were lax in executing your duties at the Edward's burial, we have a government inquiry to answer to. The bloody Department of Public Health will be scrutinising everything we do.'

'We've 'ad plague b'fore. What's to do with th' nine-foot grave and the bags o' lime? We didn't do this fa' them O'Connell kids nor Mrs. Edwards.'

'They didn't know then, you blockhead.'

'Know wha'.'

'This is not ordinary plague this is pneumonic plague. They say you breathe it in, from the air, and if you catch it, you're dead. Nobody survives.'

'Is that why ta' grave is so deep, so it don't get out into the air?'

'Something like that. Now this nurse's family has paid a handsome sum for a top-class funeral. I do not want them distressed by looking down a nine-foot grave. Have you placed the blocks in the hole so it will look six' foot when they throw the dirt on the coffin.'

'I checked it meself before me break.'

'You will keep the bags of lime out of sight until everyone has left. Absolutely everyone!' This was accentuated by a shaking of a black leather gloved fist holding an ornate walking cane.

'I have no wish for the grieving family to witness five bags of lime being dumped on their daughter's grave.'

'But that's standard fa' all plague burials.'

'I am aware of that, you dolt, but for the money they are paying they do not need to see it.'

'Alrigh', I got the picture. It'll be nice as nice can be. Flowers everywhere, the full treatment.'

'I will hold you responsible. And, unless you have a desire to go to jail, for allowing burials to proceed, without death certificates, I strongly suggest you keep your mouth shut about today's proceedings when you get to the pub.'

Ammenhauser untied his bay thoroughbred from the fence and rode back to his funeral parlour.

*

In the stables at the rear of his building the black funeral carriage and equally black horses were being polished and groomed to a shining finish. Attendants artistically loaded armfuls of flowers into the glassed rear of the carriage as the stable hands hooked up the horses. When the attendants left to change into their morning suits in preparation for the Bauer funeral the stable boys deftly moved in for a final check of the harnesses. They then walked the horses to the front of Ammenhauser's Funeral Parlour. It also didn't hurt to advertise just in case some wealthy townsperson decided they would like to make their final journey in such style.

Ammenhauser and his attendants filed out of the building and took their places on the carriage. The carriage driver checked the day's route, 'We's to go round the back of the Maryborough Hospital to the morgue. Load 'er in, put the flowers on the coffin, then round to the front of the hospital to collect the parents. You'll get the rest of 'em organised to follow the carriage up to the cemetery.

In the Mortuary Chapel the rest of the mourners will be waiting. We'll unload there and while the service is going on I'll turn the carriage around, give the horses a drink and wait for the Bauer's to come back. I take them back to their buggy at the hospital. Will that be it for the horses today?'

'That's it Eddie. Now, let's get up to the hospital.'

*

Felix and Anne Bauer waited on the footpath outside the Marybough Hospital. With the new quarantine restrictions now in place that was as close as they were allowed. A young trainee nurse walked towards them with four small packages, 'Mrs. Bauer?' She asked uncertainly.

Anne nodded, 'These are Cecelia's belongings. When Cecelia realised how ill the O'Connell children were, she packed up her belongings into four packages. One for each of her sisters she told Matron Tomlie.' The young nurse handed the packages to Felix saying softly, 'Matron Tolmie instructed me to tell you that all of these have been unpacked and disinfected, so they are safe for you to take home.' She curtsied to Anne and added, 'I'm so sorry.'

Without a word Anne took a parcel from Felix and clutched it to her chest.

'Annie dear, it's time.'

'No, Felix, not yet please.' Anne pressed the parcel to her cheek.

'The horses are getting restless, dear. We have to lay Celi to rest.'

'No! Not yet.' Anne burst into tears again. 'I cannot say goodbye yet, Felix, I just can't.' Her whole body trembled as hysteria threatened to take over.

'Annie the only thing we can do for our baby now is to give her a beautiful service. She deserves that. Please compose yourself for, Celi's sake.'

He prised the package from his wife's grip. Arm in arm they walked towards the waiting funeral party. Four glistening black horses stamped their feet and shook their necks impatiently making the black plumes on their heads dance in the breeze.

'They won't let me have her uniform, Felix. She was so proud of that uniform. Or her nightgown, she spent hours smocking that nightgown herself. Remember?'

Felix patted her arm, 'I remember, love,' he whispered.

Suddenly Anne gripped his arm in panic, 'Felix, Cecelia's flowers! Her flowers are still in our buggy.'

'It's alright Annie, I've put them in the carriage for you.

Everything is ready.'

An attendant in black tails opened the carriage door as they approached and helped the pair in. Anne picked up her bouquet of yellow wildflowers surrounding a huge white rose. She smelt the rose then sat staring straight ahead.

Ammenhauser called the party to order, and the funeral procession walked off at a sombre pace from the grounds of the Maryborough Hospital to the cemetery. Ornate wrought iron gates were open as the horses pulled the carriage along the avenue of tall trees. Their dappled leaves added the only touch of softness in the raw harshness of the Queensland sun.

Under the Mortuary Chapel the carriage came to a halt where, since 1883, mourners had sheltered while waiting for the horse-drawn hearse to arrive. When the horses had pulled to a complete stop the pall bearers stood in line at the rear in readiness to shoulder their load.

Felix took Anne's arm and together they walked to the graveside. But Anne's mind remained locked in a past where her child still lived and played. Words of admiration slowly drifted across the chasm from present to past, as Cecelia's close friend respectfully delivered her requiem.

'During her short life, she laboured with skill and patience; her noble calling gave play to qualities equally noble. And if virtues of patience, gentleness, sympathy in suffering, alertness in danger, and tactfulness in all situations calling for that quality still count to the credit of their possessor, then all those and many more adorned the character of Nurse Bauer to an eminent degree.'

Through the mist of sorrow Anne felt people shaking her hand, expressing well-meant platitudes. Then silence.

'Annie, Annie, dear, can you hear me? The service is over, we have to leave now.'

'Leave? Has everyone gone?'

'Yes, dear, you can see there is nobody here but you and me.'

'And Cecelia!'

'Please Annie, don't make this any harder for us.'

Annie looked up and studied his features. For a moment she seemed lost and disorientated until slowly recognition dawned across her face, 'I'm sorry, Felix. I was reliving the past I suppose. Please leave us for a moment. I've not finished saying goodbye yet.'

Felix bowed his head and walked slowly towards the waiting carriage. He stood rigidly next to the open door his hat in his hands. Sadly, he watched his devoted wife drop flowers onto their beautiful daughter. Tears ran unashamedly and unwiped down his chin as he turned his hat around and around by its brim.

With a shaking hand Ann pulled out one of the twenty-two yellow wildflowers she was holding. Early that morning she had picked a perfect, dew-covered bloom for each year of her daughter's life. They were flourishing near a giant Lilli Pilli tree that had been a favourite haunt of Cecelia's as a child. Slowly she dropped each flower onto her daughter's coffin as she relived each wonderful year she had been blessed to share with her child. Ann remembered the tears of happiness she shed when she first saw her perfect creation. The pride she felt when she showed off her baby to neighbours for the first time. Ann smiled as, in her mind's eye, she watched Cecelia toddle across the lawn to chase puppies, her first gurgled laugh, her first day at school.

The baby . . . the child . . . the woman . . . with each wildflower she said goodbye to them all. Finally, she relinquished to the grave a large white rose to take its place for eternity on top of the wildflowers. This was for the wedding bouquet her darling child would never have. With a wavering voice she whispered, 'My baby, you did not deserve to die this way. You did not deserve this treatment. I'm so sorry Celi, we could not protect you this time.'

Felix saw his wife's resolved was crumbling. He rushed to her side and guided her to the carriage. As they pulled away Harry Hansen and his team of men walked towards the graveside and meet up with Ammenhauser.

'Gaw'd sake, Mr. Ammenhauser,' whined Harry, 'I thought they was here for the duration.'

'Watch your mouth, Hansen. Show some respect.'

'Hey, Mr. Ammenhauser, sir, I don't get no more working here all day ya' know.'

'In a hurry to lay about the opium den I suppose.' Ammenhauser quipped.

'Not me! But what of it if I had a mind to? A working man's gotta' have some pleasure, ain't he?'

'You get more money than you are worth most times. But you did a good job with that grave. None of the family suspected that bags of lime were underneath those flowers or that the grave was 9'feet deep. Now lift that coffin up and get those blocks out of there. And be bloody careful.'

'What are ya' gonna' do?' Griped Hansen.

'I shall stand watch from under that tree and make sure you finish this job properly.' Ammenhauser started to walk off towards the nominated tree.

'Yea. Keep away from ta' plague I suppose,' yelled Hansen

to his bosses back. Ammenhauser spun around angrily, 'If that bloody yellow press gets a hold of this story there will be a lot of awkward questions. Now where would that leave you?'

Harry and his men looked at each other. Each gave a short shrug before reluctantly bending over to pick up their tools. In a short time, the coffin was laid to rest again in its new depth.

'Mr. Ammenhauser, we's ready ta' fill 'er in,' yelled out Harry.

'Thank you, Harry, but you forgot the flowers,' noted Ammenhauser.

'She don't need 'em where she's going.'

Ammenhauser walked to Harry's side and growled threateningly in his ear,

'You will pick them up carefully and drop them into the grave. Just as her mother did.'

'Alright, alright, give a man room to breathe. I'd never 'ave figured you for a sentimental fella or they must be payin' you a bundle o' money.'

Harry dropped in the flowers with exaggerated ceremony before five bags of lime were ripped open and unceremoniously dumped onto the coffin, 'Right, that's ta' lime. The lads will do the dirt shovellin'.

I've kept some of these 'ere wreaths and flowers to put on top ta' make her grave look pretty.' Said harry sincerely.

'Here's ya' stable boy with ya' horse. You may as well go now sir if you'd like. I promises to oversee the finishing touches.'

A stable boy riding a young black colt, trotted up leading the bay thoroughbred. He handed the reins over to

Ammenhauser, gave a slight nodded and headed back to town.

'Don't talk much do he?' Commented Hansen.

'Unlike you, he only talks when he has something important to say.'

Ammenhauser gathered the reins in his left hand and prepared to mount.

'Quite right, sir. Sometimes I does ramble on. But ya' gotta' admit we've done a fine job here today. Maybe a bonus for me and the boys 'ere would show your appreciation,' Hansen stroked the bay's neck as he spoke.

'You don't miss a trick, Harry. Let's see if you can keep your mouth shut, then I'll talk bonuses.'

'Nobody will hear nothin' from me.' Hansen stood back as Ammenhauser swung up into the saddle.

'Good, keep it that way and you might just earn a bonus.'

Harry stretched to get the kinks out of his back. As he did so he caught a whiff of smoke more acrid than the usual smouldering rubbish and rat carcasses. He turned towards the city,

'Ah, Mr. Ammenhauser, I think the word is out already.'

Ammenhauser turned his thoroughbred round to face the pall of thick smoke gathering above the town, 'Redolent of Sodom and Gomorrah I should imagine, Harry.'

'Ere, what's that about,' asked Harry bewildered.

'I was referring to that sulphuric stink.'

Ammenhauser raised his head high to delicately sniff the air, 'Definitely carbolic acid, chloride of lime, disinfectants, all mingled with smoke and sulphur. Well, well, I must agree with you Harry. I'd say the plague is public knowledge, but you'll still keep your mouth shut about that grave if you ever want to see that bonus.'

Satisfied that Harry's greed would override his loose lips Ammenhauser headed back to a town in the throes of a cleaning frenzy.

PRESENT DAY 15 - JUNE 7.

Sue had taken Cole to the gravesite of Nurse Cecelia. It was a clear blue-sky day with a slight breeze and a warm winter sun.

'Beautifully presented, Sue. Thank you so much. On such a perfect day as this I could almost see the events unfold before me.'

They picked their way carefully towards the shade of the Mortuary Chapel. A handsome structure with its tower and four entrances over a central axis was a unique building in Queensland and held pride of place at the centre of the old cemetery. In an attempt to keep Sue's focus away from the activities being carried out in the far sections of the cemetery he inquired, 'This is an extremely stately building, Sue. Do you know any of its history?'

'Well, I know it was designed by a Queensland Colonial architect called Willoughby Powell who had arrived in Queensland in 1872 and by 1875 had won a competition to submit designs for the Toowoomba Grammar School. In 1882 he moved to Maryborough and as well as designing this magnificent chapel is also responsible for our Baddow House that is considered to be one of the best classic heritage private homes of Queensland. Powell moved to Brisbane in 1885 and continued to design important buildings such as the Toowoomba and the Warwick Town Halls.'

'Impressive. So going back to the time of the funeral for Nurse Bauer it would seem that the possibility of plague has reached the public.'

'Yes, well impossible to keep a lid on it with the plague nurses camped outside the hospital doors.'

A movement at the far side of the cemetery caught Sue's attention. Figures dressed in khaki clothing were bending over some headstones.

'Cole, are they anything to do with you?' Sue immediately on high alert.

'Yes actually. That is why I wanted to meet you here today. As a thank you to the City of Maryborough for the assistance we have received I have allocated a team of experts to clean and mend the old cemetery headstones.'

Cole studied her profile. She was even more suspicious of his actions now and he knew there was nothing he could say or do to alleviate those suspicions. All would be revealed very soon and no doubt the earth would shake from her fury. Sue turned back to face Cole and commented icily, 'You seem to have access to a lot of people for just a medical researcher.'

'I am only one link in a chain, Sue. Now I really do have to finalise some urgent business before we all leave in a few days. Where shall we meet tomorrow?'

With mixed emotions Sue offered, 'I'd like to meet in front of the old doctor's residence. It's been turned into a hospital museum now. You'll find the details in the folder I gave you.'

Without waiting for a reply Sue spun around and headed towards her car parked under a large tree at the cemetery's decorative gates. As she walked back down the tree lined road she kept a suspicious eye on the khaki clad work crew.

DAY SIXTEEN – True Courage

JUNE 8, 1905.

'The plague full swift goes by; I am sick, I must die.'

Thomas Nashe, *A Litany in Time of Plague (1592)*

'Gentleman,' Doctor Lee Garde firmly tapped his desk to gain the attention of the doctors before him, 'Doctor Wilton Love has requested this meeting to ensure that he has all the facts that we are able to present to him about our individual involvement in the pneumonic plague outbreak in Maryborough. Doctor Love will be presenting his findings to the Premier on his return to Brisbane tomorrow.'

Doctor Lee Garde sat down behind his desk and signaled for everyone to sit down also, 'Before we start this discussion, I wish to inform you that the condition of Nurse Rose Wiles has worsened with symptoms of lobular pneumonia, cough and copious watery sputum. Temperature of one hundred and five, pulse one hundred and twenty-four, respirations twenty-three. The sputum contained enormous numbers of bacpestis.'

Doctor Love, who had remained standing, now took over the narration, 'Thank you, Doctor Garde, for bringing this meeting to order. Please accept my deepest regret for the worsening condition of your Nurse Wiles. I believe it would be an advantage for us to go over the progression of this outbreak of pneumonic plague and the order of events that have led us to this day, in the desire that we might prepare to deal swiftly with any further cases of this most deadly of diseases. Doctor Garde if you would be so kind as to preside over this assembly.'

Doctor Love took his seat as Doctor Lee Garde opened the informal inquiry, 'As Doctor Robinson attended the first victim we shall start with his observations.'

Doctor Crawford Robinson stood up and moved slightly to one corner so everyone could see him clearly. He was mildly nervous as he was not insensitive to some criticism that was being levelled in his direction containing the opinion that he personally should have been able to diagnose this disease for what it was much earlier, 'Thank you, Doctor Garde, yes, well, on Empire Day, Day One of this episode, I attended the first victim John O'Connell who appeared to exhibit all the signs of Dengue Fever. However, within twenty-four hours John died, and the attending neighbour Mrs. Edwards fell ill presenting the same symptoms. On Day Five I was again called to the O'Connell home. I arranged for the children to be admitted to hospital as they appeared to have contracted the same disease as their deceased brother. It was also my professional opinion that no matter what serious disease ailed them it would be unlikely that they would survive if allowed to remain in that indescribable filth.'

His peers all indicated agreement. Doctor Lee Garde then stood to continue the account of events, 'I called Nurse Cecelia Bauer in from her holidays to specifically look after the O'Connell children. Nurse Adelaide Wiles was the night duty nurse. On Day Eight and after only three days in hospital the lives of two of these children rapidly flickered out. Mrs. Edwards died in her home the same day. While it is true that the children had been admitted into a general hospital ward, they were kept separate. After the death of three victims in one day, we suspected a plague might be responsible. Nurse Bauer and Nurse Wiles moved the surviving O'Connell children to the isolation ward and were solely responsible for their care. Doctor Dixon, you may now go over your involvement.'

Doctor Graham Dixon remained seated but leaned forward slightly, 'I refused to sign Mrs. Edward's death certificate due to the unusual circumstances surrounding the now mounting fatalities. I applied for, and received permission for, a postmortem on her body. As the body was buried with improper haste, without a death certificate, no postmortem was performed. Doctor Lee Garde and myself reported our suspicion of plague to Mayor Dawson who, I believe, reported it to the authorities.'

Doctor Baxter-Tyrie has been impatiently shifting in his seat before he abruptly interrupted, 'Doctor Garde, may I remind this meeting that you signed the death certificate of the two O'Connell children as Broncho-pneumonia but now say you were compelled to report them as cases of plague. I have to say that I find this a most extraordinary procedure.'

Doctor Lee Garde blanketed his irritation at this onslaught under a polished façade of professionalism, 'Indeed, Doctor Baxter-Tyrie. Pneumonia was the ultimate cause of death which is a precise and accurate term for a death certificate. However, we did have a suspicion that some other disease may have caused the person to expire from pneumonic like symptoms. Therefore, Doctor Burnett Ham was informed, and the Department of Public Health dispatched you here to give us the benefit of your extensive plague knowledge.'

'I will not be dismissed so easily Doctor Garde. If indeed you suspected plague, then I can only state that it was gross negligence to send your nurses in to care for such cases with no overalls, no mosquito nets were down over the sick beds to help contain the illness, your nurses were seen to be bending over the children's mouths and they were not inoculated against plague.'

Doctor Lee Garde inhaled deeply to control his mounting anger, 'We did not have the benefit of your hindsight at the time. These children exhibited all the symptoms of pneumonia or a pneumonia type disease. Something which ordinarily does not warrant the added burden of forcing nurses to wear overalls and suffer the often-severe side effects of an inoculation with Yersin's Serum that may or may not be of any benefit.'

A chair was pushed back loudly and Doctor Henry Croker Garde commanded attention, 'Lee do not be so polite with this bombastic government lackey. His handling of the plague in Childers was so inept that I believe it requires an inquiry by the police magistrate. When Mr. Martin, the esteemed MLA member for Burrum, can die of plague without Doctor Baxter-Tyrie detecting it, then there is little hope for us here.' He accentuated his statement with a steely glare at Doctor Baxter-Tyrie, inviting a reaction.

He was not disappointed when Doctor Baxter-Tyrie responded with, 'You always were a hot head and sadly lacking in the most rudimentary of manners.'

Doctor Baxter-Tyrie stood up and they squared off like two fighting dogs, 'H.C, I do not have the luxury, sir, of being able to jump to unfounded conclusions. In my profession detailed reports on every case of plague that I send back to Doctor Ham and the premier must be supported by scientific evidence. Not local hear-say and gossip. My investigation into the death of Mr. Martin was as proper and professional as I could make it without firsthand evidence as the body had been buried before I arrived.'

Doctor Lee Garde repeatedly tapped a heavy paperweight on his desk for attention, 'Gentleman! You are both called to order. Sit down immediately.'

Both men sat obediently but remained locked in defiant eye contact.'

 'Thank you. Now on Day Ten, Doctor Baxter-Tyrie arrived in Marybrough . . .'

Doctor H.C. Garde growled, 'Yes and in two hours had made a poor family utterly destitute by ordering their home and possessions be burned to a cinder, he moved a deadly and highly contagious disease into the centre of a busy town by setting up a plague hospital, and whipped so recklessness around corners in his buggy that the townspeople have been heard to comment that such reprehensible offence should be visited with a heavy fine!'

Doctor Baxter-Tyrie's retort was as quick as a whip crack, 'I suppose you cause less disruption with that silver three-wheel horror you clatter around in.'

Doctor H.C Garde was on his feet again, 'I will have you know, Tyrie, that my De Dion is a precisely engineered machine and a piece of Australian history with two speed records to its credit. Why, it travelled four hundred miles in twenty-four hours and arrived in Warrnambool from Melbourne in the space of seven hours and twelve minutes; that is a distance of one hundred and sixty-eight miles!'

Doctor Baxter-Tyrie retorted sarcastically, 'For certain that would impress the local stable boys during their nightly symposium in the hay lofts.'

Doctor Lee Garde stood up and struck the paperweight against his desk with a resounding thump, 'Again, I am respectfully asking both you gentlemen to concentrate on our discussion and keep your personal differences aside.'

As he now had the attention of both men he sat down and continued, 'On Day Ten Richard O'Connell died and his surviving sisters Kate and May were sent to the plague hospital in town.'

He looked toward Doctor Dixon who again leaned forward to ensure that everyone could hear him clearly, 'Now, that afternoon I was called to attend May Copp, a local shopkeeper's daughter, in her home. She was exhibiting similar symptoms as our suspected plague victims. As Doctor Baxter-Tyrie was now in Maryborough I asked for his attendance also, after which he duly admitted Miss Copp to the plague hospital. As she did not worsen and survived only highlights the difficulty in diagnosing pneumonic plague.'

Doctor Lee Garde kept a stern eye on H.C. willing him to keep quiet as he continued, 'On Day Eleven, James died, and his postmortem was assisted by Doctor Baxter-Tyrie. In an effort to prevent further spreading of this disease the O'Connell home was razed to the ground. On the next day the plague nurses arrived by train from the Colmslie Plague Hospital in Brisbane after being sent for by Doctor Baxter-Tyrie. They were to escort Nurse Cecelia Bauer and Nurse Rose Wiles on the return train to that specialist plague hospital. However, our nurses refused to go and refused to allow the Colmslie nurses near them for fear of spreading this deadly infection further.'

'That!' cut in H.C., 'is dedication for you. That is true courage! Who amongst us would not grasp for comfort in the face of certain death. Nurse Wiles bravely attended to

Nurse Bauer until she died, exactly fourteen days from our first fatality. As the Colmslie nurses have the protection of the overalls and respirators Nurse Wiles has allowed them to administer to her needs as best they can now, if these are to be her final days.'

Doctor Love stood and surveyed the room, 'There are disputes aired here tonight that may well continue for months to come. Accusations and mudslinging will not save lives. When I first arrived at the Maryborough Hospital, I noted that there was unnecessary communication with the sick room by other nurses and Matron Tomlie. That no respirators or overalls were being worn, the nets of the beds were not drawn, and no screens soaked in disinfectant used. It is my recommendation that every precaution of isolation be taken in the future if any likely cases appear. I have since noted that the general rat situation appears to be well controlled, and the human population has removed or burned any rubbish with great zeal. As to exactly how and why this plague manifested itself in its pneumonic form is yet still a mystery. Thank you for donating your time tonight. No doubt an official report will be sent to you from Doctor Ham's office once I deliver my report to the Premier. Good evening, gentleman.'

PRESENT DAY 16 - JUNE 8.

Although Cole had been attentive as Sue described the events of that day in 1905, he was also aloof and distant. Something serious was on his mind, she thought, but of course he wouldn't discuss it. Not with her anyway. For the first time he did not linger to ask further questions. He gave her a curt thank you with no eye contact then strode up the road to his car and was gone.

As Sue drove out of the hospital grounds and up the main road towards the cemetery, she caught up with a major traffic jam. Vehicles were at a standstill. Some cars were attempting to turn around and go back towards town. She strained her neck out of the window to get a glimpse of the disruption. From the corner of her eye, she caught a movement above her.

'Bloody hell,' she yelled, 'what's he doing now.' In frustration she thumped her car door until it finally jerked open allowing her to stumble onto the bitumen. Pedestrians and drivers alike were staring at the sky in disbelief. A crowd was gathering in the middle of the street. Above the trees which encircled the cemetery was a giant yellow sphere billowing against the cobalt blue sky.

'You backstabbing bastard,' screamed Sue. She looked around wildly for a possible pathway to drive her car the rest of the way. But nothing presented itself.

'I'll hoof it if I have to, you snake,' she yelled at the sky before jogging around the clusters of onlookers on the footpath and congesting the roadway.

At the boundary fence of the cemetery, she slowed to a walk then stopped dead in her tracks. A yellow barricade had been placed across the road in front of a line of blue uniforms.

Police, she thought, Australian police. She recognized some of them as local cops. What has she gotten herself into? Her heart was pounding again, not from the recent run but from adrenaline as she defiantly continued on her new mission to tell Cole just exactly what she thought of him. She strode around the footpath barricade expecting any moment to have to break into a run if the police attempted to stop her. One turned his head to study her then turned back to the arguments, road rage and traffic chaos developing before him.

However, the Khaki clad guards behind the black cast iron cemetery gates were a different proposition altogether. Striding up to the gates that were usually never closed she attempted to violently push them open. At this sudden assault the guards snapped to attention but left their guns respectfully in the reverse arms position. One of them stepped forward smartly and, looking slightly over Sue's shoulder instead of directly at her eyes, barked out,

'Declare your name, Ma'am. This is now a restricted area.'
Sue was enraged at this verbal abuse, as she considered it.

'Don't you order me around you pumped up little tin soldier. This is Australia. You can't walk around with guns telling people what they can and can't do. You tell that gutless boss of yours, Cole 'bloody' Leedon, that I want to see him!'

In a whirlwind of fury, she kicked the gates and to her surprise they swung open. As the guards did not move but kept their eyes on her she walked in warily. Looking up the driveway she recognised the flaming red hair and dog collar of Chaplin Noel Howard coming towards her. As Chappie approached the guards stepped back to their original position with eyes turned towards the road. Chappie held out both of his great paws to warmly shake one of her tiny hands. With his most sincere and kindly voice he greeted her, 'Sue, please accept my apologies for our overprotective guard. Everyone involved with this project is genuine in their attempt to protect and respect the memory of Nurse Cecelia Bauer and Nurse Rose Wiles.

'They are carrying guns! You can't do that in this country or does Leedon think he is above the law?'

'Cole is in no way above the law. Every tiny detail of what he is doing here has permission from the highest authorities of this country. As to the guns you will notice they are facing behind the soldier, in no way a threat. This is called reverse arms and is used to show the very highest of reverence and mourning. Now before I take you to see Cole may I have a few words, please?'

'Why, so you can whitewash how he has used me for this, this, desecration!' She pointed to the fully inflated biosphere which now hovered above a section of the cemetery grounds.

'Absolutely no whitewashing. I have only one thing to say before we go to Cole. He needed you to fast track certain information because time is running out. But you should know that you are the only civilian in the entire world allowed to be here at this moment and that is direct orders from Cole himself.'

'You say that like he's some big wig or something.'

'He is Chief Bio-Medical Strategist in charge of one of the most secretive and important multi-national projects in the world. Wigs don't come much bigger.'

His attempt at levity fell flat as Sue remained fiercely focused on seeing Cole, 'Alright, you've convinced me I am privileged to be here without getting shot or arrested, now will you take me to him?'

Cole was waiting in the annex of his caravan-office when Sue and Chappie approached. Two somber-faced guards stood either side of the entrance but did not move.

'Stand down,' ordered Cole to the guards as Sue blew in like a tornado.

'That balloon thing is over the nurse's graves, isn't it? Why are you desecrating them?'

She went to push him with both hands but Cole caught them in midflight

'Sue, we must harvest their DNA. But they will be treated with the utmost deference . Chappie will oversee the proceedings personally.'
Cole gently lowered Sue's hands down to her side but his expression was cold and unyielding.

'Nurse Wiles and Nurse Bauer would be the first ones to give their support. Our actions here today may save millions, can you comprehend it, millions of lives. You do not believe me now, but I will make this right for you and for them. Please Sue trust me to do my job.'

'You want trust? Then tell me, just what is your job?
Cole took a step back and crossed his arms, 'Alright, remember we discussed Unit 731 and biological warfare.'
Sue snapped, 'Of course, I remember your story about torture and killing people with disease. Who in hell could forget that?'

'Indeed. Well, we believe it is happening again. Reports are coming in from an isolated political hot spot with undeniable evidence of pneumonic plague experiments being performed on the local population.'

Sue turned white and sat down in one of the fold up chairs, 'How can anyone justify killing people in such a painful manner.'

'Not just killing individuals, I am talking about decimating towns and cities, even entire countries with a disease. There are five diseases most likely to be weaponised for a bio-terrorism attack such as Anthrax which is deadly but not contagious or Smallpox for which we have a successful vaccine. It is contagious but takes prolonged close contact to spread. But the most lethal, contagious, and unstoppable is pneumonic plague. Understand, please Sue, that we have absolutely no defenses against this disease.'

Sue remained unconvinced, 'What? In this day and age? Surely there are vaccines, antibiotics . . . "

'Doctors and scientists around the world are trying but it does not respond to our most potent antibiotics and all attempts at vaccines have failed. We cannot cure it, stop it or slow it down. It survives in the air and can be easily transported and delivered as an aerosol spray. If not diagnosed and treated within twenty-four hours, it has a one hundred percent death rate. Because it looks like a flu it would raise no medical suspicions until after the first few hundreds or thousands of deaths.'

'Are you saying that if it was released in a big city like London, Los Angles or Hong Kong it could spread around the world?'

Cole snapped his fingers, 'Like wildfire. Every person who breathed in the disease would be an epidemic carrier, innocently infecting their loved ones. And we are under direct threat! Vials of pneumonic plague samples have been stolen from universities and research laboratories globally. It is such a threat that all Government Intelligence sources are working together to find the ones responsible before it is too late.'

Sue shakily stood up and gazed silently at the glistening yellow biosphere. For a while Cole remained motionless to give her time to digest the last unpalatable serving of information before loading her up with more. However, time was running out. He had to resolve this situation swiftly. He pushed himself off the caravan wall where he had been leaning to stand next to Sue. In his softest most persuading voice he revealed, 'Sue, we do have a glimmer of hope. It is crucial we harvest pristine DNA untainted by modern day pollutants. A new technique is on the horizon called Agile Vaccine. It might unlock the mystery of pneumonic plague, and these brave nurses just could be guardians of the key.'

Sue nodded almost imperceptibly. In the face of such logic for the benefit of humanity further passionate pleas against the exhumation would be futile. Her shoulders dropped as, disillusioned and overwhelmed by Cole's information, she walked away.

Cole raised his hand to get the attention of a nearby guard, 'Get Lurman immediately. I want him to make sure Sue gets home safely but he must not make contact. She has had quite enough of us today.'

With a sharp nod the guard marched off. Cole watched Sue's retreating figure as it disappeared and reappeared in the dappled shade of the cemetery roadway oblivious to the shadowing form of Lurman now her assigned protector. Chappie returned to Cole's side, 'Ah Chappie, you heard all of that?' Chappie nodded but uncharacteristically remained silent.

'All I can do for her just now is protect her from herself. Our mission must be completed, and I cannot allow her to get in the way.'

'Once she sees what you are doing for her and these nurses, I think she might forgive you, just a tiny bit anyway.' Chappie offered unconvincingly.

DAY TWENTY – Quite Heroism

JUNE 12, 1905.

'Remember me when I am gone away,

gone far away into the silent land.'

Christina Georgina Rossetti (1830-1894), *Remember.*

Doctor Henry Croker Garde looked out the window at the deserted street. It was just after midnight and although usually quiet at this time of night it had been like this all day. Terror had an icy grip on the population now that the news of the pneumonic plague epidemic was out. People stayed in their homes unwilling to go out for even a short distance.

'Let's pray that we have seen the last victim of this deadly plague,' stated Doctor Lee Garde as he read Matron Tomlie's report on the death of Nurse Rose Wiles.

Doctor H.C. Garde closed the curtains and sat behind his very heavy and imposing desk, 'You know funeral arrangements are being prepared as we speak. In a few hours she'll be in the ground. No time for formalities now, the town is paralysed with fear.'

Doctor Lee Garde noticed some letters on H.C's desk, 'So, you are going ahead with your complaints?'

'My word yes! This practice of sending so-called experts from Brisbane, as has recently been done, to such places as Childers and Maryborough, is putting the country to useless expense and worse I believe cost lives. Across the country you'll find quite as experienced and well-educated medical men as any you'll find in Brisbane.'

'Is that the extent of your complaints?'

'Lee, you know me better than that. I will not tolerate

unprofessional behavior. Doctor Baxter-Tyrie waited until June six to diagnosis pneumonic plague. Where was his microscope, I ask you? Because of this we had to send samples to Brisbane to be analysed and then with the stuff up in Brisbane it took another four days before we could get a result.'

'At least we have some good news from the plague hospital. Nurse Sprague has been receiving regular serum treatment and is improving steadily.'

'We know the serum is not effective for the pneumonic stain but either way it is good news indeed,' boomed H.C.

'Now might I suggest you get some rest? You will no doubt be attending the funeral of Nurse Wiles later today?'

'Yes, of course, practical as ever, Lee. I'll have a break now and meet you later to show our respects.'

The men got up together to leave when H.C. suddenly asked with great urgency, 'Lee, what about flowers?'

It was usually H.C. who was the tower of strength in difficult situations. The fact that his distress was perceivable in his voice reflected the high regard in which he held both Nurse Bauer and Nurse Wiles.

Lee placed a comforting hand on his shoulder, 'Matron Tomlie has taken care of those arrangements. Go home now.'

*

A crowd of mourners waited under the protection of the Mortuary Chapel in the centre of the Maryborough Cemetery. Loving family members, devoted friends and respectful workmates were drawn together for this moment in time to share their grief and their remembrances of the gentle and dutiful Rose Adelaide Wiles.

As the gleaming black horses paced smartly up the road to be relieved of their valuable cargo in the Mortuary Chapel, mourners made their way to the graveside. Haste and distance seemed to be the order of the day. No one wanted in the least to offend or upset the family, but fear was forcing an almost indecent burial, and none were keen to get too close to the coffin. Presiding over the last resting place of the daughter of his colleague Reverend Charles Wiles was the Reverend R.J. Martin.

Reverend Martin began his sermon and the subdued, nervous chatter stopped completely, "We glorify the soldier, who, amid the excitement of battle, rushes to his death, but the bravery of the soldier on the battlefield is an insignificant thing compared to the quiet heroism of those who, in the presence of a deadly disease, and with the knowledge that they themselves may fall victim to it, went steadfastly on with their appointed tasks.

To the family of Rose Adelaide Wiles it is almost impossible to find words of consolation, but I offer to them the hope that they find comfort in the affirmation that death is not the end but an open door which leads mankind into life eternal. Amen."

Quick but heartfelt condolences were offered to the grieving Reverend Wiles and Rose's devastated mother Mary Ann. Even the knowledge of the bravery of her dedicated and popular daughter could not lessen her pain. A trail of black garbed mourners moved swiftly towards the cemetery gates to disburse in each direction, leaving Rose alone.

PRESENT DAY 20 - JUNE 12.

After a scorching telephone conversation early that morning Sue had agreed to meet Cole in front of the Maryborough City Hall later that day but only because Cole had promised her empathically over and over that he could help get the nurse's story publicised. By the end of the conversation, she was cool, he was aloof, and now she was preparing for the morning ritual of driving her boys to school.

They roared out of their rooms and jostled each other to be the first into the car. Once the seat belts were clicked into place Sue pressed the button to open the roller door. In her rear vision mirror she watched the creaking door rise slowly to reveal two non-marked camouflage painted jeeps pull across her driveway accompanied by a police car.

Each jeep was driven by an extremely muscular khaki uniformed man and held as a passenger one of the German lady scientists that had been so kind when Sue had hurt herself. Both drivers got out and in perfect synchronisation and marched up to her garage door and waited. These were not quite the same uniforms as the ones she had seen at the cemetery. A small red emblem was blazoned on the sleeve and a double white cord ran through the epaulette on one shoulder. They were creased, polished and to her horror fully armed but, as she now recognised, their guns were in reverse arms.

Sue flew out of the car like an avenging fury, after an undignified few thumps on the car door.

'Get the hell off my property and tell Cole to stuff his bloody head.'

'Not Cole, Ma'am, we have been dispatched here by your

mayor. I am Smithson and this is Yohansen. You and your sons are to accompany us to city hall immediately.'

'With you carrying guns? You've got to be kidding me?

'It's our dress uniform, Ma'am.' He turned his stern face towards the police car.

'They are here so you know this is a genuine request and that you and your boys will be safe.'

'Then why are those lady scientists here and what are they carrying?'

As if on cue the two Germans hustled up the driveway carrying a powder blue suit in a clear plastic bag, a hair dryer, and a makeup kit between them. Nodding and smiling at Sue as if to cajole her into something but also leveling a barrage of information at the two men.

'Please Ma'am would you mind stepping over here near the front door.'

Sue glanced at her son's excited faces.

'They will be safe with Yohansen,' reassured Smithson. Ma'am, the German ladies outrank us plain and simple. Before coming here, they ordered us to drive into town. Next thing you know we're loaded up with what you see there.'

'They are saying that this is an extremely important occasion, and you must look your best. That stupid men do not think of such things.'

One German scientist held up the blue suit, 'She is saying it is to do with your nurses. Very important and you will be glad that you look your best. They want to help but we must be fast as everyone is waiting for you.'

Sue looked at the suit, 'Whatever that costs I can't afford it.'

'It is a gift from them to you. They read up about the nurse's story and they want to help. This is their way.'

'Ok, ok,' cut in Sue. 'If it has something to do with recognition for the nurses I'll do it. Please come in ladies.'

By now Sue's boys had lost patience and were standing near the garage door.

Smithson asked them, 'Hi boys, so this is your uniform. You both look fine except for those shoes.'

Yohansen bent down and proceeded to spit and polish. In a few moments four scuffed shoes had been transformed into shop window condition. When the front door finally opened again the boys were lost for words.

'Mum, you look like model,' gasped Simon.

'No, a movie star,' yelled Josh.

'Well, thanks guys. Now let's get and see what all this is about.'

Smithson walked to the front jeep and held open the door for her, 'Ma'am it is not my place to say this, but you look a knockout.'

Simon had struck up an animated conversation with Yohansen who picked the boys up one at a time and placed them in the back seat.

'You know what?' Piped up Simon. 'I've never seen a gun like that, not even on TV.' Simon was in great awe of the lethal weapon.

'It's a beaut son, shoot the eye out of squirrel at 500 paces and . . .'

Sue's glacial gaze stopped Yohansen dead in his tracks. Regaining composure he quickly added, 'Sorry, young sir, regulations prohibit me from fraternising with civilians while on duty. Please buckle up and remain silent.'

Once Smithson had settled the two German scientists in his jeep the police car lead the cavalcade down Sue's Street.

A crowd had now gathered all the way to the city hall where the police car and the jeeps pulled up. In front of Sue's jeep, a red carpet led to a large item on the city hall green shrouded at the moment in a red velvet cloaking. Television cameras lined up on both sides of the carpet and a radio station booth was giving a live running commentary.

Sue ran her gaze over the dignitaries waiting on one side of the red carpet. She recognised the mayor, some local councilors and a sprinkling of members of parliament. On the other side was a troop of men in unfamiliar uniforms. In front of these stood Chappie dressed in his solid black chaplain's outfit with gold crosses on the collar holding a vermilion leather covered bible.

Next to him stood Cole in civilian clothes smiling uncharacteristically like a Cheshire cat as he stepped forward and took Sue by the elbow saying softly, 'Before you berate me again, but this time in front of live television, may I suggest you sit down first and listen to my dedication speech. You will not be disappointed. And by the way, you look stunning.'

Cole guided her to seats next to Josh and Simon and then stepped up to the microphone. Behind him on either side of the red cloaked statue stood two huge bouquets of yellow wattle and eucalyptus leaves. It was a perfect blue Australian morning. Azure sky, golden sun, the flash of vibrant colours through the trees as local parrots searched for nectar.

Suddenly the background stillness became quite noticeable. for the center of town in the morning. There were no cars, no bikes or trucks compliments of the barricades around the town center to keep noise to a minimum.

In that quiet, sunny moment Sue closed her eyes and

allowed herself to imagine what this beautiful, elegant town must have looked like over a hundred years ago when this city hall was being opened for the first time. A slight tap on the microphone by Cole snapped her back to reality.

'Maryborough, your authorities have welcomed this tribute to be placed in your most honored of positions as the heart of this wonderful city. This act will be a light of inspiration to towns and countries around the world to not let all that is destructive overwhelm us. Bring unselfish deeds and brave people back into the light. Allow their actions to inspire us to greater things. They have shown us that humanity has the power to heal itself and throw off the shackles of destruction and oppression. With acceptance and quiet dignity these two brave nurses forced an outbreak of the deadliest plague on Earth to die with them. For this selfless action they have received very little public recognition or appreciation until now. As a thank you to the gracious city of Maryborough for your contribution in helping us understand this disease we offer you this ever-lasting tribute.'

A gasp of admiration escaped the crowd as the red velvet cloaking fell to the ground revealing a magnificent statue of John, James, Ellen, Richard and Joanna O'Connell, Nurse Cecelia Bauer, Nurse Rose Wiles, and Mrs. Letitia Edwards. When the admiration died down Cole continued his speech,

'On this beautiful morning, we gather in this quiet sanctuary to pay our respects to the unoffending and innocent victims of this most virulent and deadly disease. Although now silenced by death they still have something to say. To every doctor who has remained silent behind the safety of his profession. To every council that has failed to keep its town clean and vermin free. To any government that places policy before its people. These victims are saying that we must not be concerned merely with how they died but in the way they lived.

They were not only victims of a lethal disease but of an uncaring society that allowed children to live in such squalor and a health system that kept a deadly outbreak a secret until almost too late.

When angels of mercy die in the course of their duty it should not go unrecognized. To Nurse Rose Wiles and Nurse Cecelia Bauer may you always remain the guiding lights of this city.'

DAY TWENTY-FOUR - Accusations

JUNE 16, 1905.

The plague full swift goes by: I am sick, I must die.

Thomas Nashe, *A Litany in Time of Plague (1600)*

Roses of every colour were in the full flush of bloom in the magnificent gardens of the Maryborough Hospital. Striding purposely up the gravel pathways from different directions were Doctor H.C. Garde and Doctor Lee Garde. No social pleasantries were exchanged as H.C. immediately launched his tirade, 'I tell you I will not tolerate the blame for these plague deaths being laid at the door of our local medical men as implied by the Commissioner of Public Health.'

'H.C. really no blame has yet been leveled at any of us.'

'You have read those damned letters from Ham's office and the newspapers are stirring up the pot as well. It will not be long before those high and might officials start writing their reports with us made out to be country hicks.'

'But we know and everyone in town knows that each and every doctor here who dealt with this plague outbreak has an exemplary medical background.'

'I know that of course but that blithering Doctor Baxter-Tyrie is reporting to Brisbane that he was unable to procure a microscope in Maryborough which you know is utter rubbish. There is a perfectly good one at the School of Arts and I am told one of our doctors offered him the use of theirs. Had he bought his own microscope at least our nurses might still be alive.'

'Really H.C. we do not know that for a fact.'

'I believe it to be the case. A so-called plague expert without his microscope is like a surveyor without his theodolite; bloody useless!'

'Yes, I have to agree with you there,' said Doctor Garde.

'Lee, you should know that I am demanding the Department of Public Health sets up an inquiry headed by an uninterested and competent man, not just an internal Department whitewash. Our Police Magistrate would be highly suitable as a responsible person in which the people of Maryborough can have confidence. I would then expect a state of affairs will be disclosed which will put the blame, if any, on the correct shoulders.'

'As to the diagnosis of plague H.C. we accepted pneumonia on the death certificates of the first cases.'

'As did the illustrious plague expert Doctor Baxter-Tyrie until we ALL knew better on June six. You and Doctor Graham Dixon reported your suspicion of plague to Mayor Dawson on May thirty first. He in turn immediately wired the Commissioner of Health in Brisbane who sent out Doctor Baxter-Tyrie as a matter of the greatest emergency who arrived on June second.'

*

While Doctor H.C. Garde was outlining every grievance he held against Doctor Baxter-Tyrie the object of his scorn was being driven to the train station for his journey home to Brisbane by Doctor Penny.

'Doctor Penny, I am well aware of the accusations your Doctor H.C. Garde has leveled at me. In my report to Doctor Ham and the Health Commission I will be noting the following observations.

Firstly, that on my arrival on June second the question of plague was raised but no definite evidence was available to the naked eye.

Secondly, when I visited the children in hospital I was struck with the utter disregard of ordinary precautions. No overalls were being worn; the mosquito nets were not down, and the nurses were bending over the children's mouths. I urged Doctor Lee Garde to have these precautions instituted at once.

Thirdly, that I did not accept the cases as proved plague until the sixth is quite true. There was no scientific clinical or postmortem evidence and there was no microscope to make a diagnosis which is an outrageous condition of affairs in a hospital of that size. Diagnosis of pneumonic plague is notoriously difficult. Confirmation can only be made by bacteriological tests. It is my opinion that Doctor H.C. Garde has failed to realize that the bacilli cannot be detected with the ordinary lens of the average microscope. For bacterioscopic examination a somewhat expensive oil immersion objective is absolutely necessary and none of this was available to me in Maryborough.

Fourthly, that I was fully seized of the importance of prompt and decisive action is proved by the fact that I caused the O'Connell's house to be burnt down. I also ordered the ward that had been occupied by the plague victims in the General Hospital be shut up and all of its contents burned on the same site. At the home of the unfortunate Mrs. Edwards, I ordered the fumigation of the dwelling and clothing and the destruction of the bedding.

Fifthly, I ordered the specialised plague nurses to come to

Maryborough immediately. Every action I have taken has been by the book and to the exacting government health policy guidelines.'

He took a breath and turned to his travelling companion to ask, 'What say you, Doctor Penny?'

After a pensive moment Doctor Penny answered, 'I am privy to the suspicions of Doctor Ham that the plague may have been carried from the Childer's outbreak to Maryborough in substances such as horse and cattle fodder as has been recorded in other countries. I am, of course, specifically referring to reports during the recent Boer War when British troops unknowingly transported infected horse feed by rail across South Africa dropping off feed at various railway stations as they passed. In so doing they spread the plague over a large area of the country.

But of course, in this instance with no warning signs of an impending outbreak such as sick or dead rats and no persons reportedly afflicted with the telltale signs of enlarged lymph nodes it is impossible to determine where or how this disease was able to manifest itself only in its pneumonic form.'

Doctor Baxter-Tyrie gave a slight nod in agreement, 'And of course you are aware of the delicate political tinderbox on which I am perched. It placed on my shoulders the responsibility for the possible financial ruin facing the state of Queensland if a premature and unproven announcement of plague were to be reported. I had to be one hundred percent sure, with scientific proof to back it up, that plague was the cause.'

'Just so,' agreed Doctor Penny. 'An untenable situation I understand. You may or may not be aware that the same pressure you are facing seems to have been too much for Doctor Challands after the Childers's incident as his resignation will be made public next month.'

Doctor Baxter-Tyrie was not surprised at this news, 'More likely forced to resign and I fear my head will be on the chopping block when I return to Brisbane.'

'How so?' inquired Doctor Penny.

'Under these fragile negotiations with the New South Wales premier to lift the plague embargo on Queensland's produce our government cannot be seen to be negligent in any manner. You have seen the mudslinging in the newspapers. Our government must be publicly seen to be doing something, no matter if it is fair or not, so I believe I am next in the firing line.

As Doctor Penny dropped off Doctor Baxter-Tyrie at the Maryborough train station little did they know that soon Tyrie would be moved to Cairns as the Health Office there and his position appears to have been replaced by Doctor Penny.

PRESENT DAY 24 - JUNE 16.

At the cemetery gates Sue studied the change in the landscape. All the caravans along with the bio-sphere equipment had been packed up and hauled away. Every headstone, ancient and new, was gleaming white and in full repair. Shrubs were clipped and the lawn manicured another gift from Cole's men to the town of Maryborough. Millions of flowers now lined the pathways to the gravesides of Cecelia Bauer and Rose Wiles. Today was a very special ceremony to honour the nurses' contribution to society.

It would all be happening soon but just for a moment she wanted to gather her thoughts and take in the peace. She walked over to the dedication stone which was laid in remembrance of the Kanakas and other races that helped in the founding of the Maryborough township. *Gone Home to the Land of our Brothers* it stated. She wondered if any of these had also contracted the plague and died unattended in the canfields or even disposed of in the Mary River. Those were harsh times for these people.

Cole put up his hand to halt the honour guard at the gates. He wanted a chance to talk to Sue alone. From a distance he called out, 'Sue, I am so glad to see you.'

She watched him stride towards her in those garish boots. As the sun hit the overly-elaborate gold trims they actually glittered. He was next to her now asking, 'Am I forgiven just a little bit?'

'I suppose I have to thank you for the statue. I don't know how you had it made so quickly but it is the most magnificent thing I have ever seen.' Sue acknowledged reluctantly.

'It was your idea and your sketches. You are a celebrity now.

There will be television interviews, radio talks, probably even a book deal and everyone will know the story of the Maryborough nurses. Now you are famous I am sure you have another crusade to pursue?'

Cole's astute question caught her off guard. She hesitated before answering, 'Ah, well actually I have been thinking of doing just that.'

'At the end of today's ceremony, we will all be gone but I hope you will keep in touch via email?'

'Sure, if you would be interested. But today is a very special occasion and I can't believe how beautiful you have made this place look.'

'We are all here to honour your nurses in the best way we know how. It is my sincerest hope that they can see us from wherever they are now. And did you notice the date, Sue? I was very specific about the date?'

'Yes, the quarantine notice was finally lifted from the Maryborough Hospital. So, you did read all of my notes.'

'I read every word over and over. I thought this would be a fitting date to put an end to this episode just as it did then.' He held out his arm for Sue to take, 'Sue, are you ready now?'

Cole gave the signal for the guard of honour to precede them. Three uniformed men in white gloves snapped to attention in front of Cole and Sue. Each man carried a large vividly coloured flag on a gold flagpole. An Australian flag, a Queensland flag and the ornate bottlebrush emblem of old Maryborough. Three more men in immaculate uniforms took formation behind the flag bearers. Sue noticed that they were minus their guns. She looked behind her to see the other soldiers now flanking each set of two guests. None were carrying their customary weapons.

Cole followed her gaze, 'It is an iron-clad traditional for these formal events that weapons be carried. Sue, you have absolutely no idea of the arguments I had to break with tradition and order no weapons to be carried. I know how you feel about them, so I was determined to show you in a practical and public manner how much your contribution has been appreciated.'

'Thank you, Cole.' Sue said almost demurely.

Behind them were the mayor and local dignitaries, high ranking military personnel, ambassadors, doctors and researchers. In unison they followed the trail of huge flower baskets leading to the nurses' graves.

Cole took up his position at the lectern placed midway between the two gravesites, 'Before I hand over the proceedings to our Chaplin for the final dedication service it is my duty to clarify to you why we are today. The use of bio-terrorism weapons generates a moral revulsion in most people and yet in the last century and into this one, certain countries have deliberately weaponised the world's deadest diseases with the result of millions of deaths.

These horrific events have demonstrated the ease with which a motivated group can perpetrate an act of bioterrorism. International groups concerned with preventing a bio-terrorism attack have found at that least seventeen countries today have active biological weapons programs.

Several dissident groups have the skills necessary to cultivate lethal pathogens and the will to deploy them. We have limited ability to predict or prevent such an attack or manage the consequences. Even today using modern laboratory procedures, at least two to three days would be required to identify the organism from culture isolates for pneumonic plague. In that respect little has changed in over a century when these valiant nurses took charge of the care of the unfortunate O'Connell children. As no effective vaccine exists even today against pneumonic plague it is crucial that we gain an understanding of this lethal and highly contagious disease. We have gathered over the past few days samples that will be invaluable in protecting medical workers and military staff who will be at the frontline of an attack.

Hopefully we will be able to deploy a vaccine for the general public should it ever become a necessity. For the glimmer of hope these nurses have given us we can only offer our most humble thanks. Our Chaplin, the Reverend Noel Howard, will lead us in a formal dedication service.'

Chappie took over the microphone and immediately launched into his service, 'Lord, in Rose Wiles and Cecelia Bauer you gave to this world two wonderful children. They were not on this earth long, but they lived a meaningful life. No greater tribute can be paid, and no greater epitaph can come to their relatives than the knowledge of the service their daughters were performing when they died.

Because of their dedication to duty and their compassion for suffering their lives were taken also. They could have walked away but they would not turn their back on a family of dying children. This great unselfish act should stand out as a symbol of human altruism for all generations. Please join me in prayer.

Dear Cecelia and Rose, we offer you this final prayer. May the flight of our Lord's angels recognize you as one of their own and comfort you during your eternal rest. Good night, our Angels of Mercy. *Requiem æternam dona ei, Domine, Et lux perpetua luceat ei, Requiescat in pace, Amen..*'

At the completion of Chappie's prayer the crowd, now armed with handfuls of multi-coloured flowers distributed by the honour guard, threw them into the air.

Sue smiled as the beautiful final tributes carpeted the ground and the two graves, 'Rose and Cecelia, I hope you can see this,' she whispered in the gentle winter breeze.

o 0 o

CHARACTER BIO'S AND PHOTO

BAUER, Cecelia Elizabeth. Born April 28, 1883. At age twenty-two left nursing to prepare for her wedding. She was called back to the Maryborough Hospital to care for the O'Connell children. Nurse Bauer and Nurse Wiles immediately isolated the children, allowing no one to enter the ward. Food and other necessities were left outside the door. She cared for the stricken youngsters continuing her selfless vigil even after watching the youngsters die a terrible death. She died on June 6, 1905. *(Image: findagrave.com)*

BAUER, Felix and Mary Ann. Cecelia's parents married in 1877 and had ten children. Mary-Ann passed away in 1908 and Felix in 1910. Walter, their eldest son, took over running the property in Blackmount, Tiaro, until his death in 1958.

Back in the 13th plus centuries these beak like masks were worn by doctors filled with aromatic herbs and flowers in an futile attempt to prevent them catching the plague. Over the centuries this image has become synonymous with the plague and death.

BAXTER-TYRIE, Doctor Charles Campbell. He was the government Health Office and plague specialist at the time of the Maryborough outbreak. Born in Rattray, Perthshire, Scotland in 1871 he graduated from Edinburgh University in 1892. In 1904 he migrated to Queensland with his family and was appointed MB Master Surgeon of the Colmslie Plague Hospital, Brisbane. In 1905 he was sent to Maryborough to investigate a report of contagious deaths. A year before he had written a very comprehensive *Report of an Outbreak of Plague in Queensland during the first six months of 1904* which was published in *The Journal of Hygiene*, July 1905.

On his appointment as Health Officer in Cairns he moved his family there and set up private practice. He was a founding member of the Cairns Masonic Lodge in 1907 and in 1908, was elected the first president and commodore of the Cairns Aquatic Club of which he was a founding member. An active sailor, he took part in competitions and judged club events on social occasions. In 1909 he was appointed Quarantine Officer and in 1910, an Examining Officer under the Federal Invalid and Pensions Act. In May 1910, Dr Tyrie travelled to the tent town of Oaks Rush (Kidston), 400Km from Cairns, to investigate an outbreak of typhoid. Oaks Rush was the site of a new mineral field with many recent arrivals coming from the New Guinea goldfields. His investigations showed it was a particularly virulent form of 'black jack' malaria. He had the power to order the township site be moved and stringent hygiene procedures be put in place. Fourteen people died in the outbreak. Tyrie was a man of action and was heavily involved with the local cricket club, athletics club, the newly formed tennis club, the Rifle Club, Oddfellows, Swimming Club, Caledonian Society, Cairns-Mulgrave Jockey Club, Cairns Citizens Band and the Kuranda Trout Stocking Association.

He was a founding member of the Cairns Chamber of Commerce and was president of the local ambulance. He appeared regularly on the roster to hear cases in the Police Court and was frequently called upon as an expert witness.

As Government Medical Officer he was required to journey to Palm Island, Chillagoe, Kuranda, Port Douglas and Yarrabah involving travel by boat, train and overland bush track. In 1912 he was appointed the Sub-district Naval Medical Officer to the Cairns Naval Forces and Medical Officer to the new Cairns Harbour Board in 1913. This same year he ran for Council and was successful.

By early 1915 he resigned all positions in Cairns, as he had been ordered to undertake war service. Appointed Naval Surgeon on board the *Una*, he left for Rabaul in New Guinea. *Una* was the former captured German boat *Komet*. **His legacy to Cairns and the Far North was his ground-breaking work in malaria and infectious disease control**. He is remembered with the naming of Tyrie Close, a street in the suburb of Earlville, Cairns.

In February 1917 he died in the Cootamundra Hospital, N.S.W., from an attack of pneumonia and pleurisy at just 46 years *(Image: State Library of Queensland)*

DAWSON, William. Maryborough's highly respected mayor during the pneumonic plague outbreak. Born in Cleyton-Le-Moore, Lancashire. He was Superintendent of St. Stephen's Presbyterian Church in Maryborough from 1891 to 1897. At various times he operated a funeral service, a bookseller's and stationer's office. He was a very public-spirited man and was mayor of Maryborough on four occasions. Dawson was instrumental in securing a large donation from George White for building the city hall. He passed in 1922 aged 84. *(Image: State Library of Queensland)*

DIXON, Doctor Graham Patrick. He was the general practitioner to Mrs Letitia Edwards. He was born in Brisbane in 1873. He graduated as a university medalist and prizeman in surgery, anatomy, and physiology. During 1910 he studied in Scotland, France and Switzerland and returned to Brisbane as a consulting surgeon in Wickham Terrace. In 1914 he was once of the first officers ashore at Gallipoli where he served until the evacuation. In January 1916 he was appointed lieutenant-colonel and commander of the 1st Light Horse Field Ambulance at Heliopolis. After four years continuous field service he was appointed C.B.E. (Commander of the British Empire). Dixon returned to Brisbane as one of the leading surgeons at the Children's Hospital. He was a founding fellow of the College of Surgeons of Australia and in 1922 was president of the Queensland branch of British Medical Association. He held many trophies for horsemanship. He died in 1947 age 74. *(Image: vwma.org.au)*

GARDE, Doctor Henry Croker. He was the resident surgeon of the Maryborough general hospital at the time of the pneumonic plague outbreak; a position he had held since 1884. **He was considered one of the most skilful surgeons in the Commonwealth.** Garde was born in Cloyne, Cork, Ireland on February 9, 1855. His grandfather Doctor Abraham Colles had won international acclaim for a bone fracture treatment. H.C. was a licentiate of the Apothecaries Hall Dublin and the Royal College of Surgeons Edinburgh. He was a ship's doctor before arriving in Maryborough in 1879. In 1886 he married, and the couple had a son and four daughters. An undeniably brave man he received a bravery award from the Royal Humane society of Australia in 1893 for rescuing a man drowning in floodwaters. This was his second such award. In 1911 he served in Egypt and on hospital ships as a major. He was an official at the local race clubs and established a stud at Tandora on the Mary River with a reputation of breeding fine horses. In 1932 he died in Maryborough age 77 of cardiac failure. *(Image: Queensland Politician Stock Photo)*

GARDE, Doctor Henry Lee. Was the medical superintendent and resident surgeon at Maryborough Hospital at the time of the outbreak. He was born in Cork, Ireland in September 1876. At the age of two years, he moved to Australia with his parents. He was the half nephew of Doctor Henry Croker Garde causing frequent confusion as both men were born in Cork, both were medical officers at Maryborough hospital, and both had served as Aldermen on the Maryborough council. He married in 1904, and the couple had four children. He received much unwarranted criticism from Brisbane over the pneumonic plague outbreak but was held in high esteem in Maryborough. He died unexpectedly in 1925 when only 48 from acute cholecystitis, peritonitis and toxaemia causing heart failure. *(Image: couriermail.com.au)*

HAM, Doctor Nathaniel Burnett. He was the Brisbane-based Queensland Health Commissioner at the time of the pneumonic plague outbreak. He was born in 1865 at Smythesdale, VictoriaIn In 1900 he was awarded an M.D., with distinction, at the Université Libre de Bruxelles, Belgium. 1901 Ham was appointed Queensland's first commissioner of public health and is considered the father of Queensland's Department of Health. Ham tackled the problems of bubonic plague, food adulteration, sanitation and infectious diseases. His *Report on Plague in Queensland, 1900-07,* received worldwide recognition. At a time when the role of fleas in transmitting plague to humans was being evaluated. In the area of food adulteration, **his initiatives led to Queensland's being the first Australian State to draw up food standards laws.** Ham introduced compulsory notification of diseases, including tuberculosis and hookworm. Ham was founding president of the Queensland branch of the Life Saving Society of London (Royal Life Saving Society) in 1905. His enlightened attitude set the direction for venereal disease legislation principles that are followed today. In 1913 returned to England. In 1914 on the outbreak of war he joined up as medical officer in the Irish Guards. At the end of the war he investigated allergies and pioneered inhalation therapy for chest diseases. In 1954 Ham died in Orpington Hospital, Kent, aged 89. *(Image: trovenla.gov.au)*

HASTINGS, William. The heartbroken fiancé of Cecelia Bauer ordered a marble headstone from Italy which was put over Cecelia's resting place. He moved to America where he was possibly killed in a work accident.

LOVE, Doctor Wilton Wood Russell. Was born in Hollymount, Ireland in 1861. His family migrated to Queensland in 1862. At Edinburgh in 1884 he graduated M.B., Ch.M. Love was a pioneer on bacteriology, pathology and the use of diathermy and x-rays. He frequently assisted the Department of Police in microscopic forensic work. He had been president of the Queensland Medical Society and the Queensland branch of the British Medical Association, a founding fellow of the College of Surgeons of Australasia, and served on the Senate of the University of Queensland. He died at his historic home, Bulimba House, Brisbane (now heritage listed) in 1933. *(Image: State Library of Queensland)*

O'CONNELL, May. Once released from hospital May was found wandering the streets and taken into police custody. She was sentenced to six years at the Nudgee Industrial School in Brisbane to learn a factory trade.

O'CONNELL, Kate. Kate went with May and two nurses to Brisbane. There she gained employment in the Brisbane Convent as a domestic.

PENNY, Doctor John Alexander Cairns. Maryborough's Government Medical Officer at the time of this outbreak was born in Dublin in 1861. His medical training was completed in Dublin. He arrived in Maryborough in 1886 and took up the position of medical officer for the A.M.P. Society. He was married in 1886 and fathered two sons. Penny was a first lieutenant in the Maryborough Naval Brigade from 1888 until 1910. His wife drowned in January1916 and Penny died in April 1916.
(Image: Maryborough and Burnett Historical Society Inc)

ROBERTSON, Doctor Crawford.
He was the Maryborough Municipal
Health Officer at the time of the
pneumonic plague outbreak. And the
first doctor to attend John O'Connell.
Born in Queensland in 1871. He was
unjustly accused by some for not
diagnosing the notoriously difficult to
detect pneumonic plague immediately.
He was in fact extremely more
conversant than most with infectious
diseases and was in no way at fault. In
1912 he and his wife moved to Sydney where he set up a
surgical practice. He accepted the position of Honorary
Gynaecologist for the Sydney Hospital. He died in Sydney
in 1966 aged 93. *(Image: State Library of Queensland)*

RUHLE, John David. He was the fire brigade
superintendent in charge of burning the O'Connell home to
ashes. Born in Brisbane in 1853 and arrived in Maryborough
in 1875. He was a colourful character in the town and was
a founding member of the local fire brigade. Ruhle was
especially proud of his horses and bought only the best stock
which he displayed each year at the show. His death in 1916
was under the most unusual circumstance. A postmortem
reported that death was caused by arsenic poisoning. When
Ruhle was found dead one coat pocket contained a bottle of
rum and in the other pocket a similar bottle containing ant
poison. It is suspected that he simply drank from the wrong
bottle!

SCHAFER, Henrietta Mathilda. Not a happy life for such a benevolent soul. She married in 1912, but her husband was charged with bigamy and ended up in prison. In 1940 she married again to a widower who had four young sons. Two years later her husband died of a burst appendix leaving her to raise his children alone. She died 1944 age fifty-eight from cancer of the uterus.

THOMPSON, Doctor Ashburton. In 1905 was the president of the New South Wales Board of Health. On June 10 he lifted the twelve month ban on Qld produce.

TOMLIE, Matron Agnes. She was appointed Matron of Maryborough Hospital due to her exemplary work at Toowoomba Hospital. At the age of 93 she attended the unveiling of the fountain dedicated to Nurses Bauer and Wiles at the Maryborough City Hall on August 13, 1966.

WILES, Rose Adelaide. Rose attended the O'Connell children with Nurse Bauer. She was taken ill on June eight with the same symptoms and died on June twelve, 1905 at midnight thereby extinguishing the threat of a the pneumonic plague epidemic with her death. Rose was 28.
(image: findagrave.com)

BIBLIOGRAPHY

Baxter-Tyrie, Doctor Charles Campbell. *Report of an Outbreak of Plague in Queensland during the first six months of 1904* was published in *The Journal of Hygiene*, Vol. 5, No. 3 (Jul., 1905), pp. 311-332.

Boccaccio, Giovanni. *Decamero (1353.)*

Cole, L.A. *The Eleventh Plague* (2002).

De Foe, Daniel. *The Journal of the Plague Year* (1722).

Department of Public Health. *Report of the Commissioner of Public Health.* (August 23, 1905).

Earnshaw, Dr. P.A. *Unwept, Unhonour'd and Unsung* (1966).

Fletcher, C.B. *Bubonic Plague: Outbeak in Queensland and New South Wales.*

Gregory, Helen. *A Tradition of Care (*1988).

Ham, B. Burnett. *Report on Plague in Queensland: 1900-1907* (1907).

Matthews, Tony. *River of Dreams – A History of Maryborough & District* (1995).

Maryborough, Wide Bay and Burnett Historical Society. *A History of Maryborough 1842-1976* (1976.)

Nashe, Thomas. *A BLitany in Time of Plague* (1600).

Patrick, Ross. *A History of Health and Medicine in Queensland 1824-1960* (1987).

Ransom, Steve. Plague, Pestilence and the pursuit of power. The politics of global disease (2008).

Rossow, Lind A. *The Saddest Chapter (2009)*.

Shakespeare, *Venus and Adonis* (1593).

Thearle, M. John M.D. and Jeffs, David M.R.C.P. *Plague Revisited The Black Death: An Account of Plague in Australia 1990-1923* (1994).

China Daily Newspaper. *Horrors of war haunt old soldier.* (Yoshio Shinozuka Unit 731). September 18-19, 2004.

Holman Christian Standard Bible, Psalms 91 (2004).

http://ststephenshospital.com.au/about-us/our-history
The Australian Dictionary of Biography - http://adb.anu.edu.au/biography/dixon-graham-patrick-5981

The Australian Dictionary of Biography - http://adb.anu.edu.au/biography/love-wilton-wood-russell-7245

The Medical Journal of Australia. Vol. 1 – 53rd year. Sydney, Saturday 12, 1966.

ABOUT THE AUTHOR

Nerida is an investigative journalist who, in the early years, researched political unrest issues throughout the Pacific islands and New Zealand. This experience gave her an insight into the struggles of First Nations people.

Once back in Australia she specialised in gathering information for government and justice departments, current affairs television shows, animal rights groups, authors and filmmakers.

Presently she is working on a series highlighting the achievements of extraordinary pioneer women in Australia.

NEXT BOOK:
BATAVIA'S WOMEN: Slaughter, Sex and Survival

If you would like to keep in touch you can follow her on the Facebook page of Nerida E Marshall author

WRITING WORKBOOK COLLECTION
by Nerida E Marshall
Available on Amazon books

CREATIVE WRITING – EXCITING WRITING
Learn the fundamental techniques to spellbind readers.

SCREENWRITING FOR BEGINNERS
All you need to know to write and market your first script.

WRITING MAGAZINE ARTICLES FOR PROFIT OR HOBBY
Tap into this lucrative and unlimited market.

WRITING ROMANCE STORIES –THAT SELL
Learn the rules for the multi levels of today's romance stories.

WRITING FOR CHILDREN – NOT AS EASY AS IT LOOKS
Learn the strict guidelines for successful children's stories.

RHYMES, RHYTHMS AND STORYBEATS
An advanced study of techniques to enhance your stories.

THE HEALING POWER OF WORDS
Pleasant words are healing to the bones.

WRITING LIFE STORIES AND FAMILY HISTORIES
Create written treasures for your family.

www.ingramcontent.com/pod-product-compliance
Lightning Source LLC
Chambersburg PA
CBHW051130020726
47501CB00005B/1442